White Rain

by

S.J.P. Rubin

White Rain

Park Rubin Media
99 Pinehurst Rd.
POB 436
Canyon, CA 94516

Contact: parkrubinmedia@gmail.com

Cover Concept: Sally Park Rubin
Cover and Book Design: Ed Rubin
Cover photo: NASA
Back Cover Portrait of Sally: Sam Rubin

10 9 8 7 6 5 4 3 2 1

ISBN-13: 978-0-9796807-2-4 CreateSpace Edition
ISBN-10: 0-9796807-2-7 CreateSpace Edition

For CD, whose jambalaya of life stories form the hard luck backbone of this tale. One who has never lived it could truly know the sweat, grit, and ruin of this region of the Bayou Teche, especially after the devastation from Hurricanes Katrina and Rita. But, dear C, with your spicy roux, the fire of my pen, and a story worth telling, I hope the flavor of these places and events has been honored and brought to life.

~ ~ ~

WHITE RAIN

1 Popo Cole

4:30 a.m., September 23rd, 2005, the first hint of
sunlight whispers across the deep indigo dome of the
pre-dawn sky. A late summer blanket of heat lies over
the sugar cane field near the edge of a liquid quagmire
swamp which rises up from a tributary of the
Apachalaya Basin where Popo Cole's tin-roofed shack
sits on a slight knoll among the burnt sugarcane stalks.
The black sugar tar, a thin layer of schmear, smelling
and tasting like burnt toast, clings tenaciously to
anything and everything in its smokey path. An
invisible hermitage hidden deep within the Bayou
Teche of Southern Louisiana, this one room is evidence
of the scattered Cajun diaspora living out its eternal
punishment in this meager land, so rich with secrets of
survival known to few. Chiggers and termites, fire ants
and mosquitos, roaches and nutria, herons and
goshawks, wind and rain, in the swirl of morning
vapors—fog, mist, and sugarcane soot—the shack is its
own story. Its cyprus planks are cobbled together on
bastions of cane stalks with frayed Sunbeam Bread
plastic bags, tied one to the other in tight knots,

lending color—bright red, yellow, and blue—to the otherwise unadorned terrain. Seasons of watermarks on the boarded sides, like tree rings, show evidence of floods and hurricanes...water up, water down, water sideways. When there is wind, its tenuous walls heave like a woman in childbirth, while the torn thin edges of the bright plastic tick like dried leaves on window panes. But, on this morning, stillness is all.

Inside the shack, Popo Cole Boudreaux, maybe all of sixty (he doesn't really know when he was born), lies, fully-dressed, wearing a short-sleeved cotton plaid shirt from the mercy box of Our Lady of Perpetual Help Church over in Delcambre, and a pair of stained men's slacks from a suit, won in a bourré game, having formerly belonged to Antoine Charles, the janitor at Chez Giselle's gay cabaret dance bar out on Highway 78, near where Pangay's Honky-Tonk and Bingo Palace sit at the crossroad to New Iberia.

Popo lies snoring on his cot. His muddied tie-boots sit just beneath his muscled girth. His thick arm hangs down, his strong fingers touching the boards where linoleum has peeled to reveal the underfloor, dusty and rotting except where the staples hold it down.

A voice calls out to him in the darkness. "Popo, bring me home."

Recognizing his daughter's sotto voce, a voice like sheer white muslin wafting softly from a clothesline in a gentle breeze, Popo Cole opens his eyes quickly and stares through the darkness. Like a jaybird's ungainly squawk in response to the cooing of a dove, his guttural voice breaks the morning silence with a throaty hack. "Celestine...."

"Bring me home, Popo. Today's the day." Celestine's command is clear and certain and he, her father, of course, will do her bidding. This is the day.

Disheveled and grisly, Popo Cole is a Cajun "traiteur"—a conjuring man. On his stomach sits a sandbag-weighted ashtray filled with Camel cigarette butts, smoked one after another the night before. As he shifts, an empty Schlitz can falls to the floor, taking its place in the tin halo of cans surrounding his cot. His bare feet swing firmly around, finding their way into his boots in the darkness. This is easy for a Cajun man. Men like him have night vision—their hands able and willing to reach into any dark place to find what's there —like frogs for fried frog legs dinner or fresh catfish caught live, sans hook—bare hands only—from a Bayou bog...and pull it out to the light of day.

He reaches for a votive candle and lights it with a match. The dim illumination reveals ointments, salves, herbs in mason jars with frog parts, cooking oil and mint. In another jar...eucalyptus bark, resin-colored cooking oil and basil. In another...mint, Vic's Vapor Rub, and lard. Alongside all this are drying herbs, holy water, holy oils, jars of Anisette—a fig-pear moonshine which he calls his *cough syrup*, and an array of candles on which are written incantations to the Holy Mother Mary. Beside the potions sits Catholic paraphernalia (a picture of The Last Supper, yellowing with antiquity, a standing wooden cross, and some Mardi Gras beads) and a picture of Celestine in fifth grade, holding up a baby bird she'd rescued, its wing broken by the jaws of a feral cat. There is also a rosary, worn from years of use. There is a one-burner camp stove. All this sits on simple TV trays lined up precariously like jaybirds on a slumping high wire.

He lights the stove and heats up a day-old pot of coffee inside a double-boiler. He spikes the coffee with hickory, chicory and tobacco, rendering the coffee forever black like coal. *Mississippi Mud*, they call it.

A symphony of cicadas and crickets tune up their contra-tenor bassos on cue, filling the air with a loud, yet lulling, s'wrrpzch' s'wrrpzch' s'wrrpzch' sound as the sun burns a path towards the horizon. These are the sounds of le Bayou au matin.

Popo Cole turns his transistor radio on. The voice on the radio cracks: "Hurricane Tracker... czrrrchzt... czhhhzzhhh...Rita...czzzh... hundred and sixty miles south...czhhhzzhhh...City. Winds at. czhhzzhhh... czhhhzzhhh......dred-and-forty miles per czzzh. Get your ...czhhhzzhhh... at Beaufort Fish and Tackle and Rouses Market, 6403 Highway 18czhhzzch... East. ...czhhhzzhhh..."

He takes a handkerchief and dips it in the hot coffee, wipes the sleep out of his eyes. He puts baking soda on his teeth and rubs over them with his index finger, spitting the stains out the front door. Lastly, he scrapes his tongue with a spoon, then rinses it with some spit and chicory. He dons his talismans—a cross of Jesus, a scapula bearing the Trinity. A red chili-pepper colored nutria rat tooth hangs on a string around his neck, next to the scapula. He places a medal of St. Christopher in his sock, crosses himself, stands up, pours the hot coffee from the pot into a rusted tin cup, and swallows it in gaping gulps. He taps the radio off and steps outside to the outhouse to relieve himself. He wipes himself with a corncob. A pail to the right holds the fresh corncobs and one to the left holds the soiled ones.

Emerging from the outhouse, while zipping his pants, he's met with the lumbering slog of a two foot long nutria rat. Without missing a beat, Popo Cole reaches into his shack, grabs his machete by the door, sharp from working in the cane fields, and whacks the head off the nutria in one fell swoop. He looks up and says to his Lord, "Merci por le diner, Chèr." He reaches down, grabs the dead nutria carcass by its bleeding neck and flings it up on the tin roof. He takes the head and drops it into a crawfish net, hanging off the side of the outhouse.

Then, he grabs his tool satchel by the door, three shovels and a sledge hammer and walks out along a path out of the swamp.

He looks up at the sky, with fingers of amber, pink, and magenta reaching across it. Sunlight now licks the tops of the sugarcane stalks. A slight wind breaks the cricketing somnolence. On the distant horizon, a thicket of storm clouds gather, a red glow. He grunts and sets out walking Eastward across the cane field towards Celestine.

2 Belle Boudreaux

Miles away, number three-forty-seven Atchafalaya Swamp Road, like a tired old hound dog, lists to its side in the early morning heat. Located on a shell-strewn side road off the main highway, this little stilted slave shack, left over from before the Civil War and fairly in need of a fresh coat of paint, stands inside a backwood boundary of the inner flood plain of the Mississippi Delta and on the outer edge of the McIlhenny Tabasco Plantation, its acres of red and yellow pepper fields sitting atop a submerged mountain of salt the size of Mt. Everest. All the homes here are built above ground on account of the seasonal flooding.

The outside of three-forty-seven Atchafalaya Swamp Road, however, belies the inside. Three steps up from the cracked sidewalk and across a small rickety front porch, you enter what could only and aptly be characterized as a model home. When you step over the threshold, the living room is immaculate. The smell of Pine-sol, Clorox, and magnolia sachet permeate the air. The walls are painted an amber tone with white woodwork. On the windows are scalloped shades with tasseled shade pulls. In front of the shades are beige marquisette sheers with cream brocade. The curtains, hand-sewn and lined, are of a fleur-de-lis pattern with a scalloped valence along the top.

On one side of the living room sits a simple dining room table, polished to a high sheen, giving it the look of an expensive piece of furniture; but, it's not. The same goes with the end tables next to the couch, lacquered to look like mahogany. Matching lamps on them bear a decoupage of autumnal leaves with acorns. The lampshades have gold and russet brocade trim at the top and bottom. Vanilla- and cinnamon-scented candles adorn the end tables, adding a warm ambient accent to the tiny room. The sofa—russet with Earth tones—sports hand-embroidered chenille throw pillows in olive and chocolate. All this is the handiwork of Belle Boudreaux, Popo Cole's estranged wife, a white woman in her mid-fifties who works as a "Maid of Mercy," which is a glorified title for a coffee lady at the local funeral parlor, and who, also, cares for her three grandchildren—fifteen-year-old Beau Landry, sixteen-year-old Trent, and thirteen-year-old Felicia.

The Landry-Boudreaux abode is what you call a shotgun shack, meaning that if you shot a bullet through the front door, it would travel clear through every room, one behind the other and out the back door. With a wall of heat already pressing against its exterior, four members of the family sleep.

Belle's alarm rings 4:30 a.m. She deftly taps the sound off, swings her legs out of bed and launches into her morning routine which consists first of removing white cotton gloves she's worn all night to ensure that the Vaseline she put on her hands and fingers the night before (after her bath) has appropriately softened the skin, making it look and feel young. She folds the gloves neatly onto her night stand, then makes her bed, its corners so taut and precisely fitted, you could bounce a dime off it. Then, she heads into the kitchen to put on a pot of coffee.

The kitchen is painted daisy yellow with white woodwork. Priscilla curtains adorn the windows— yellow and orange mushrooms and butterflies are embroidered into a white valence, scalloped with organdy trim. The shade pulls are yellow with orange filigree. In front of this proscenium surrounding the window frame are marquisettes with hand-painted mushrooms and daisies. One window holds a large air conditioner to keep that one room cool. The room sports a used washer and dryer, stove and refrigerator, all painted with heat-resistant white enamel. On the cabinets are luscious floral arrangements—more mushrooms, more daises, jonquils and forget-me-knots. Glued to one mushroom is a little mouse waving, as if to say: Welcome to Belle Boudreaux's kitchen!

A large pantry, so clean you could run a white glove over its shelves and contents, houses canned goods and dry goods, most of which have been opened and resealed from the bottom—save the cans which are habitually opened from the bottom, so that they can be replaced on the shelves after their contents are emptied. The empty cans and boxes, neatly lined up like soldiers on Belle's paper-lined shelves, serve as props, to give the illusion of a well-stocked kitchen for the occasion on which a nosey neighbor or relative comes by to "check in."

Belle puts on her coffee. While the coffee is brewing, she prays—her daily conversation with God—chanting like a Benedictine nun. *Oh, Lord Jesus grant me the strength to get through this day and do Thy will. Have your angels watch over my angels. Let no one tease or hurt Trent and Beau today. Help me serve as a light to bring the balm of Gilead and comfort to the bereaved people I will serve today at my job. I ask that you anoint me and guide my words and my actions with an open and loving heart. Relieve my grandchildren of the bondage of hate. They need a little light and so do I. Hail Mary full of grace.* She hums and rocks in a trance-like fashion and when the water comes to a boil, she stands up, stays on the note and pours her first cup of coffee. *Oh, I just love the feel of a hot cup of coffee in my hands. Lord, I don't care how hot it is outside. MmmmMmmm, this is niiiice....* She drinks it, enjoying the silence before the chaos of grandchildren and her busy work day.

She immediately washes the cup, even though she will be using it again shortly, a habit inbred in her from childhood where she would be punished severely if she'd so much as left a cup on the counter or a glass in the kitchen sink. She heads to the bathroom. A water stain bleeds through a patch in the ceiling—something she and Beau have tried and failed to repair, covering it over like liquid paper with many typographical errors. *I know, Lord, you are doing your best to protect me and my family. I'm just not going to look up at that dingy ceiling.* She casts her gaze from the ceiling to what she can control, feeling pride in the washed, pressed, immaculate white eyelet curtain on the little bathroom window.

She burns a scented candle on the sink and looks at herself in the shiny mirror. The few items in the bathroom cupboard—a make-up mirror, shampoo, combs, hairspray—like the kitchen pantry, are perfectly lined up, as if waiting to be called to active duty. Belle pulls the make-up mirror from the cupboard and places it on the back of the toilet tank. She sits side-saddle on the toilet seat and proceeds with her morning make-up regime, applying cleanser with the one towel that is stained. She uses a cotton ball for her moisturizer and concealer, then pats her face in quick little slaps to insure that the concealer is evenly distributed under her eyes and in the folds of the skin on each side of her nose. For her foundation, she has a palette on which she mixes a shade perfect for her. She applies it to her entire face and neck with a make-up brush, so that there are no visible make-up lines. Then, she blots that layer with rice paper to ensure she's taken up any excess moisture. A finishing powder—a combination of tinted talc, Cornsilk, and a touch of apricot rouge—is applied with a make-up brush, designated for that purpose. Then, she powders her entire face with a finishing coat and dusts off the excess. Finally, she applies a rouge that glows on her cheeks and the canvas is set.

On to her eyes...with the dusted eyelids, she applies a cream base on the eyelid and with her artist's brush, puts a burnt sienna in the crease, blending upward. A small patch of light cream is applied below the brow. She waves her eyeliner pencil over the flame like a conductor waving a baton to a well-tuned orchestra. The eyeliner is a mahogany to match her hazel eyes. In one perfect stroke, she makes the line, one to each eye. She next applies three coats of mascara to her eyelashes, allows them to dry, and then pinches them into an upward curl with an eyelash curler for an ever-alert and seductive flutter. The denouement of this artistic endeavor comes with the pin that meticulously opens up space between each lash. Eyes done.

She heats up her lip pencil in the candle flame, lines her beautiful French mouth with a cranberry color, applies a merlot lip stain, applies talc on top, brushes off the excess. *Oh, I just looove this raspberry color! And it's almost out of season. But, I can wear it one more day.* Lips done.

She then closes her eyes, inhales, and sprays her face once with *White Rain* hairspray as a protective impenetrable sealer, so that no matter how much perspiration or how many tears, she'll stay exquisitely perfect.

All the make-up and make-up utensils are put back exactly in the order in which they were used. She unpins the eight pin curls from the front of her hairline and puts the bobby pins back into their container, all in the same direction, and puts the container back into its place. She gently tousles the curls so that they cascade around her face. After the birth of her daughter, Celestine, she lost a small patch of hair at the crown of her head, so she's taken to wearing wiglets which she's designed herself—having cut this one from the back of a salt and pepper wig, she sewed in a medium champagne grey to its center. To the front, grey, silver, and champagne highlights match her own hair...perfectly. With brute force, she bobby-pins the wig right past her own hair, so that it could withstand a Gulf gale wind. Combing her own hair in front over the wig where she's loosened the pin-curls, she pinches the curls into place and sprays a copious amount of hairspray to hold it all together.

Having done her nails the night before, she inspects them and sees that there are one or two in need of a little touch up. She heads back to the kitchen for her second cup of coffee. Then, Belle applies a touch-up coat of polish to one of the two nails in need of repair. She holds one hand in front of the air conditioner to let the first coat dry while she drinks the coffee with her other hand. And, then, switches to apply and dry the opposite hand. She heads back to the bedroom.

Belle takes a moment to examine her make-up in the mirror. All set. *Now, for the fun part.* She wrestles with her all-in-one girdle, adds a waist cinch over it. *I need to sew this a little tighter, the elastic is getting tired and I do __not__ want my zipper to buckle!* She pulls on her panty hose, and checks her lipstick one more time. She sprays on perfume—a scent that no one in the city wears...a mixture of florentine, spice, and lily-of-the-valley...that always turns heads. *Perfect, the smell of highborn women...lilacs and lily-of-the-valley...not like that dreadful Jean-Naté!* And, last, but not least, she pulls on her dress, attaches the clip-on earrings she'd picked out the night before. She stops to balance them, unclips and re-clips until they look right. From the tiny dime store mirror on her closet door, she examines the whole picture. *Oh! I know... Today I will wear a symphony of pearls.* On a long thin chain, little pearls sit at the gravitational bottom, each pearl, an "add-a-pearl," with a memory—a birthday, Christmas, Mother's Day. Her grandson, Beau, would never forget to give her one more to add on. "Someday, Mawmaw, you'll have a whole string of Mikimoto pearls!" Then, she pulls on her perfectly polished closed-toe pumps with two-inch King Louis heels.

Back to the kitchen, she pours another cup of coffee, inspects the touch-up coat on her nails. *I better set up the ironing board.* She sets it up in front of the air conditioner in the kitchen. *I can feel it's going to be hot.*

It's already 90 degrees.

3 Belle's Grandchildren

At 6:30 a.m., Beau's alarm clock goes off. On his side table, lined up, are five bottles of cologne—Paco Rabon, Estée Lauder's *Pleasure*, Polo, Calvin Klein and Hugo Boss. Like his grandmother, he immediately makes his bed with military precision, pulling the cream chenille bedspread over the top and leaning the one accent pillow with an embroidered quail on it squarely against the pillow at the head of the bed. Above the bed board is a painting that he checked out at the library—a Rembrandt. He revolves the artwork every two weeks when his library loan comes due. But, in between, he studies the greats—Raphael, Michelangelo, Botticelli, Caravaggio....

Beau goes to the kitchen for his first cup of coffee —black—and takes it with him into the bathroom. He uses an electric razor because his acne is so enraged by the sugarcane air and dampness that his face always feels as if it's on fire. He carefully places little pieces of toilet paper where he's cut himself. He takes extra care on the scabs on his face where he was recently pummeled by Purnell Buford, a neighbor boy who has taken it upon himself as his Christian duty "to punish queers." *And you are a faggot, sissy-boy, Beau Landry-Boudreaux.* Beau winces at the thought of Purnell's voice and his damning words.

He waits for the blood to congeal. Then, he puts astringent on his acne. With some acne cream that his grandmother has mixed to be his perfect shade, he dabs it onto the zits and scars. And, like his grandmother, pats his skin in sharp little taps to blend it all in perfectly, leaving no lines between his natural ruddy skin color and the color of the shade.

He then takes an eyebrow pencil and fills in his eyebrow to cover the loss of hair from scarring on the bone above his eye, a constant reminder of his deadbeat father. All put together, this routine creates for Beau a teflon mask of resiliency. *All is well*, he assures himself, his confidence bolstered by pride transacted and earned through survival as a motherless and a fatherless gay-boy in the Bayou Teche.

Belle, who's just finished ironing her granddaughter's dress, sews a label at the back of the collar, to make it look new—Ralph Lauren, taken from the suit-dress of the corpse of Estelle DuBois, whose husband owned the rice mill across the Bayou. *No one will know this is a used dress, not even Felicia.* "Beau, come get your brother's pants." She hands Beau his brother Trent's creased pants. "Thanks, Mawmaw." Beau heads back to his bedroom. Beau lays Trent's crisp pants on his bed and dons a starched white shirt he'd ironed the night before. He chooses a cologne. Sprays it amply onto his neck and heads to the kitchen to cook breakfast.

He cracks enough eggs into the poaching pan to feed the family. Then, as he's done since he was five years old, before his father, Rightly Landry, left the family for good and before Celestine, his mother, passed on to Heaven, he mixes instant grits, boiling water, butter and milk, and lets it all simmer on the stove. He mixes in imitation bacon bits because they make his brother Trent happy and that matters more to him than almost anything.

When he was a little boy, Beau would run from the kitchen to his Momma Celestine for the next instruction for cooking dinner which Celestine, who had taken to her bed, delivered deftly to him, despite her protracted faint on account of Trent's mental retardation prognosis. Beau's first cooking *tour de force* was noodles with hot dogs and bacon bits. Trent loved it. Felicia picked at it, mainly because Beau had cooked it. Beau was always amazed at how at even a mere three years old, Felicia was already a colossal bitch.

"These are cooties!" she would snarl. On the verge of tears, Beau would look to his mother to come to his defense.

"Lagniappe," Celestine would say.

"Lagniappe, Momma?"

"Yes, Beau, honey, *lagniappe* is a Cajun cooking word. It means that little extra something you add that makes the meal special, like sugar in tomato bisque. Now, you just go tell your sister that it isn't cooties. It isn't even bacon. It's lagniappe. She won't understand right now. Someday she might. No matter. It's lagniappe, just the same."

It was the first time that Beau understood the unique way in which his mother communicated to him and him alone—that she could count on him utterly and completely. And, in exchange, she always had his back.

Beau would apply the lagniappe paradigm to his acting auditions in years yet to come. There, he would certainly give the adjudicators that little extra sumpthing and, to the dismay of his classmates at Juilliard, he'd always get the parts.

One musky evening, Rightly returned from the off-shore roust-about for his landfall fuck. Lucky for him, Celestine was already basking in bed where she had stationed herself for the last three weeks to ruminate about Trent's diagnosis, leaving it to Beau to care for his big brother and little sister. Rightly arrived with the usual swagger, standing there, flexing his deck-honed muscles in the back-lit doorway. Celestine's heart always skipped a beat when she saw that man, as selfish and cruel as he was. As handsome as Little Joe Cartwright, once she could smell his sweat, her resistance broke down like the ladies at the local quilting circle to sugar cookies on tea trays. Celestine took Rightly into her bed, let him do his manly thing and when he was done, as sweetly as she could muster, she broke the news to him about Trent. Without saying a word, Rightly sat bolt upright, swung his legs off the bed, stepped into his pants, buttoned his shirt, donned his cap and walked out. Forever.

On the way through the kitchen, he knocked the table over which had been set for morning breakfast by little Beau before going to bed the night before. All the dishes broke. It was about then that Celestine finally realized how utterly belligerent Rightly had become, if he hadn't always already been so and she hadn't noticed, or worse, had simply denied a truth that was as plain as day to everyone else. She tucked herself under her covers and cried privately until there were no tears left to come out.

Hearing the crash, Beau went to the kitchen and began to clean up the mess. When Momma Celestine did not come out, he knew it had to be bad. Before he checked in on her, he made sure that neither Trent or Felicia would be touched by a single shard of glass. After awhile, Celestine, red-eyed and with her lips pursed, entered the kitchen and said to Beau, "Popo Cole taught me how to feed my family from crawfishing. But, Beau, I can't be out in the swamp hunting for crawfish all day with Trent!"

Beau, ever the earnest five-year-old, "Momma, I can help you. We'll make it work."

"Beau, honey, I need you to go to school, so that one of us has the learning we need to keep this family going."

"Momma, I've got lagniappe!" Beau smiled.

And, for the first time since Trent's diagnosis, Celestine laughed out loud. "Well, Beau, honey, I reckon you do."

~   ~   ~

On this morning, like every other morning since he was five years old, Beau mixes the grits with artificial bacon bits and sets it out in individual bowls. Four eggs, immaculately poached, one egg each on top of a mound of grits.

Beau goes to wake up his older brother, Trent. Trent, in Calvin Klein pajamas, sleeps with his beloved Wile E. Coyote stuffed animal. "Trent, it's time to get up."

"I be up. Tank you bery much please."

"Trent, I got grits with bacon bits."

"Oh, tank you bery much, Beau!"

Beau wakes his sister, Felicia. She has on her white gloves with hand cream and pink sponge rollers in her hair. "Felicia, it's time to get up." Felicia doesn't move. Beau touches her shoulder. "Felicia, wake up."

"Don't touch me," she snarls. His stomach knots. He grits his teeth and backs out of her bedroom. And he soldiers on with the school morning routine.

When she finally emerges from her bedroom into the kitchen and spies the usual breakfast—with the bacon bits mixed into the grits, he chirps, "Stick to your ribs!"

Trent, of course, loves his breakfast. Felicia predictably picks at hers, mostly because Beau made it. Beau looks at her plate. "Don't you be wasting that food, Felicia. Mawmaw works hard to feed us. If you don't like it, put a little salt on it." Felicia, saying nothing, sneers at him and chews her food like a cow chewing its cud, its jaw dropping heavily on the downbeat and her face miserably grimacing on the upbeat.

Beau dresses Trent, helping him on with his pressed shirt and pressed khaki pants. Trent talks about a movie he wants to see, "Can we watch the scary movie on TV tonight? It be bery important. It be scary movie. We be watching that." Beau ties Trent's shoes. Beau had taught Trent the word "horror" and gave him a subscription to *TV Guide*. So, Trent would scour the *TV Guide* for the word and latch onto it, wanting to watch anything that had that word associated with it.

"That sounds good, Trent. I'd like to watch that movie with you."

Trent goes into the bathroom and brushes his teeth. When he is finished, everyone else comes in. Trent sits on the commode and Felicia sits on the edge of the bathtub, her feet in it. Beau takes care of Trent, flossing his teeth, shaving his face, fixing his cowlick. Mawmaw Belle takes care of Felicia, taking the pink sponge curlers out of her hair. As each one is removed, Felicia's hair unfurls into sausage curls. Belle has a place for each sponge curler—the small, the medium, and the large. But, before she puts them into their slots, Mawmaw Belle precisely and skillfully pulls the stray hairs off them.

"There you go, Trent," Beau admires Trent's face. "All shaved. Now, I'm going to gel your hair."

"Please tank you bery much," Trent obliges and rocks in approval.

Belle separates each of Felicia's sausage curls, separately blows each one dry, splits each one open to where it looks like luscious windblown, curly hair. Felicia, with her back to them all, winces. If her eyes were knives, her grandmother and brothers would be filleted by now.

"I need my hair done today, Mawmaw!" Felicia barks at Belle.

Beau bristles at Felicia's shrill yap.

Belle is not going to let her patience be tried at this hour of the morning. "I rolled your hair last night after being on my feet for twelve hours, Felicia. And your new dress is clean and pressed fresh this morning. You will be the prettiest girl on the Sugar Court." *Dear Lord, the devil has hardened poor Felicia's heart. I pray that Jesus and the angels melt that Devil from it.*

"Trent's almost done, Mawmaw," Beau assures Belle in an effort to smooth the tension.

Belle tries to stifle her annoyance with Felicia by stating the obvious. "I can't unroll and set your curls any faster without them getting tangled. That would just defy the laws of gravity."

"Thermodynamics!" Beau interjects.

"What Beau said, honey."

"That's right, Mawmaw," Beau lords it over Felicia with his extensive vocabulary, even though he's mixing metaphors and he knows it. He also knows that she doesn't know, and that's all the power he needs to win. Although Belle and Beau laugh heartily, Felicia is not amused.

"If y'all keep laughin', I'm gonna' tell that Beau's wearing make-up today"—Felicia's ornery nature spews at fever pitch this morning.

"It's acne cream," Beau insists.

"It's make-up," she retorts.

Belle chimes in, "I mixed a little medium tint to match Beau's shade. I think it matches more evenly, don't you?"

"Boys don't wear make-up."

Not only can Beau out-stubborn Felicia, but he can pretty much beat her at anything. She's just not that smart. And *he* is whip smart.

"Well, you know what Dolly Parton says?" he quips. "A barn always looks better with a fresh coat of paint." Belle and Beau guffaw at the delicious levity that breaks the tension in the room. Belle grabs the *White Rain* hairspray.

"Alright everybody. Lean over."

The Landry-Boudreaux grandchildren all dip their heads in unison while Belle copiously sprays their meticulously prepared 'do's.' As he bends over, Beau notices his mother, Celestine's, reflection in the mirror.

Celestine speaks to Trent, "You look handsome today, Trent."

"Tank you bery much, Mudder Dear."

Celestine tells Beau to fix Trent's cowlick.

Beau obliges and tweaks Trent's cowlick, "Yes, Mother Dear."

Belle casts Beau a sideways glance. She heard it, too. Celestine smiles approval from the mirror; Trent's hair is now perfect. Belle and Beau smile at Celestine, with a look that says, "It's so nice to be appreciated," the Dead being the ones who truly fathom life's kinder souls.

Felicia doesn't have the gift to see spirits. "Why are you sayin' that?"

Everyone ignores her.

The school bus outside grinds and takes off. Trent jumps up from the bathroom and beelines out the front door.

4 The Bus Driver, Mr. Thibodeaux

Trent runs after the bus. Beau bolts after him.

Holding the screen door open, Beau yells, "Hurry, Mawmaw! He's past the boucherie. Go! Go! Go!"

Belle drops everything into the tub where Felicia sits. "You'll have to crimp that bow yourself, Felicia." Felicia calls after her, "You can't go, Mawmaw!"

But Belle is already out the door.

Beau grabs Trent's school book, lunch bag and Trent's Special Olympics medals which Trent won for bowling and swimming. He follows on Belle's heels.

Felicia stomps to the front door, screaming, "I am Miss Junior Sugar Cane Queen!"

Backing up the car, Belle calls out to her, "Lock up, Felicia! And leave the key under the rock by the drain pipe."

Felicia leans on the door jam, seething, and preening her hair. "You messed up my bow!" It's little sugar cubes dangle like car dice beside her heavily mascara'd eyes. "They're taking pictures of the Royal Sugar Court this morning and I better look good..."

But no one is listening to her. "...or I'll make sure Beau gets it."

Beau keeps his eyes on Trent as Belle throws the car into gear and backs out of the driveway.

"Don't lose sight of him, Beau!"

"I've got my eyes on him, Mawmaw."

Belle weaves in and out of cars, honks and flashes her lights to get the bus driver's attention. Running like a marathoner, Trent's singular focus on catching his school bus makes him impervious to the passing cars.

"Dear God! Someone's going to run over my little angel."

"Mawmaw, just keep your eyes on the road. I've got my eyes on Trent."

To his left, Trent passes The Boucherie, Shirley's "Perm, Curl & Tint," Maynard's Superette, and a couple of run down slave shack houses. On the right, Shadows-on-the-Teche Nursing Home, Monroe's knife-sharpening shack, some other shotgun shacks, and the Easta' Egg shacks—painted lime sherbet, lemon sherbet, and strawberry sherbet. You can't miss 'em.

Finally, the bus stops ahead of them at a stop sign. Trent bangs on the back of the bus, his eyes squinting from the fumes coming out of its tailpipe. Belle's car screeches up behind the bus. She storms out. Trent gets on it as if nothing has happened. Beau follows Belle and runs onto the bus to check on Trent. Trent has already taken his usual seat.

"Trent, are you alright?"

Unfazed, Trent looks ahead, "I not miss bus, Beau. I go to school. Mama be happy. Tank you very much, please."

"Trent, Mama's not here."

Trent insists, "Mama's in the car."

"You promised, Trent."

"I not say we talk to Mama."

It's no use arguing with Trent.

Beau scans the bus, narrowing in on the de la Houssay girls who have recently taunted Trent about not having a girlfriend. With Beau's right hand on Trent's shoulder, his left hand goes up into a point and fixes it on those girls. The wrath of Beau is worse than the wrath of God—a gentle reminder, so Trent will not have to suffer on the way to school at the hands of these evil teenagers. The de la Houssay girls look back at Beau, their mouths smirking as if they'd just eaten rancid cheese. They roll their eyes and look out the window. Beau stares after them for an extra minute, to insure they will NOT do what they think they want to do.

Then, Beau changes his focus back to Trent. "Don't run off like that again, Trent. You scared Mawmaw Belle."

"I not miss bus. Tank you very much, please."

Beau, still shaken, hands Trent his lunchbox. He fusses with Trent's collar to help himself calm down. Then, he reaches into his pocket and pulls out Trent's Special Olympics medals. "Here, Trent. Don't forget your medals." He puts them over Trent's head and adjusts how they hang over his shirt.

"Oh, Beau, tank you bery much please." Trent holds his medals with one hand.

Then, Beau heads to the front of the bus, Belle leans in. "Is Trent alright, Beau?"

"He's okay, Mawmaw."

As he looks at the mullet-haired blonde de la Houssay girls, Beau thinks to himself...*must have fallen asleep with peroxide...white trash...They'll be pregnant by the time they're fifteen. Why. Am. I. Even. Thinking. About. This!?* He snaps out of it and turns to go.

Without a hair out of place, Belle takes her focus off Trent and onto the bus driver. "Thank you, Beau. Now, if you don't mind, I just need to have a little moment with the bus driver. Oh, Mr. Thibodeaux, would you kindly step out here?"

Mr. Thibodeaux, a short round-bellied man, steps out of the bus. All of 5' 6", he's a compact, barrel-chested fellow, with a large French nose, blue eyes, and a line for a lip. He's also balding, has thick hands, and wears an all-in-one blue men's jumpsuit. The lapel says: "Romero's Air Conditioning"—his other job. On his feet are brown Florsheim's, no socks. And he's got a small forest of hair growing out of his ears.

Belle smiles, sweet as pie, at Mr. Thibodeaux, "If you would just kindly close the door, Mr. Thibodeaux."

Without a word, Mr. Thibodeaux reaches behind him and shuts the bus door.

"Now, Mr. Thibodeaux, how many years have you been driving our Trent on your bus?"

"J'n sais pas, chèr," he replies.

"Nine years, Mr. Thibodeaux. You've been driving my grandson and picking him up in front of my house every school day for nine years."

"Dat sounds right," he replies, "Miz Belle."

She looks up to the Lord for guidance and takes a deep breath before continuing. "Mr. Thibodeaux, has my grandson *ever* not been waiting for you?'

"Mais non, I don't tink so," Mr. Thibodeaux looks at the ground like a schoolboy himself.

With the keen analysis of a great prosecutor, "And, Mr. Thibodeaux, in all those years, has my grandson, Trent, *ever* missed a day of school?"

"Mais non."

"That is correct, Mr. Thibodeaux. Trent has never missed a day of school."

"Mais yea, even when his mama died," Mr. T. admits.

Belle feels the pain in her chest—everybody knowing about Celestine—but she recovers her dignity quickly and, then, Belle's sugarcane syrup demeanor turns on Mr. Thibodeaux like a bull seeing red. "Well, then, Mr. Thibodeaux, the next time my grandson is not waiting at his bus stop, I will expect you to knock on my door ... You know, neighborly like, to double-check if he's not coming. Is that clear?"

Mr. Thibodeaux shifts uncomfortably from one foot to another. "Yes'm." He jingles the change in his pocket and turns to go.

Belle Boudreaux then asks, "Just one more question, Mr. Thibodeaux." By now, Mr. Thibodeaux has resigned himself to Belle's upending.

Beau steps off the bus and asks, "Mawmaw, did Mr. Thibodeaux hear Trent banging on the bus?"

"No'm. I didn't."

Mawmaw Belle steps between Beau and the bus driver, "I'm almost done visiting with Mr. T., Beau. Go to the car."

Beau slinks back, but watches with rapt attention. Celestine sits in the back seat, arms folded, smiling.

With all the charm ever granted a Southern lady, Belle turns it on. "Mr. Thibodeaux, when it comes to working with children, one needs to have eyes in the back of one's head, don't you know?" And, then, with pitch perfect venom, she goes in for the kill, "And if my grandson *ever* has to run after *your* bus again, by the sweat of my bra straps, I will walk immediately to your wife, Mildred, and have a talk with her about how your pick-up truck is always by Shirley's 'Perm, Curl & Tint,' when you have no hair." She smiles. "Have a blessed day, sir."

Mr. Thibodeaux stumbles back onto his bus, closes the door, and drives off.

As the bus passes, Belle and Beau in the front seat and Celestine, sitting in the back seat, wave. Trent looks ahead, like any other day riding the bus to school.

"Now, I'm late for work, Beau. And look at me!"

"You look beautiful, Mawmaw."

She gets out her rice paper and blots the perspiration from her brow and from right above her lip. "Ooo, Ooo, the powder under my arms feels like icing, Beau!"

In the car mirror, she dabs a little talc on her lip-liner. Beau watches with rapt attention to her method of application. She smiles, "See, Beau, you add a little talc to keep the color from running up the creases in the skin above the top lip. The heat will melt this stuff in no time. But, the talc creates a layer between the moisture of your skin and the moisture in the air."

Then, to Celestine she says, "Another battle won, Celestine. ...with a little bit of lagniappe."

The car radio announces: "Hurricane update. Rita is a hundred miles due South of Morgan City."

Beau looks out the window and up at the sky. "Storm's coming up fast, Mawmaw."

Belle returns her lipliner to the make-up pouch in her purse and puts the car in gear. "I don't even know why they bother having a school day. They're going to close early when the hurricane hits." She lets Beau out at his school. "Now, y'all bring Trent over to the Azalea when school gets out."

"Yes, Mawmaw. I promise I will."

Belle drives off. Celestine sits silently in the back of Belle's car, gazing up at the gathering sky.

5 The Azalea Funeral Home

The Azalea Funeral Home sits on a quiet street two blocks off Highway 41, a stone's throw from a wide loop in the Bayou Teche rivulet. The stately home was built in 1863 by prominent Civil War General P.G.T. Beauregard, a graduate of West Point—who, after many successful battles, including the battles of Bull Run and Shiloh, was among the first of the Confederate officers to recognize and admit that the South was simply outmanned by the military power of the North. He and his commander, Joseph E. Johnson, encouraged Jefferson Davis to end the war and, thus, the two gentlemen soldiers—Beauregard and Johnson—bore witness to the formal surrender of General Robert E. Lee to the Union's General Ulysses S. Grant at the Appomattox Court House in the foothills of the Blue Ridge Mountains near Lynchburg, Virginia.

Upon P.G.T. Beauregard's return to Southern Louisiana, he adjusted his sights to commerce, becoming an executive for the newly thriving railroad enterprise. He also engaged himself in launching the Louisiana State Lottery, which grew to become one of the more corrupt institutions in the State's history. So blackened with graft was the lottery that it earned the nickname "The Golden Octopus." With the money from this—shall we say—lucrative enterprise, he built the house which is now occupied by the Azalea Funeral Home.

A late-Victorian antebellum home with ample parlors for visiting the Dead, it probably once had a beautiful view. But now, P.G.T. Beauregard's post-Civil War opulent residence sits between Pop's Gas on one side, with an expansive cement parking lot on the other, and across from the Rosemont Memorial Park cemetery near the Eastern bend in the rivulet. There is a small cemetery in the back for those who, for one reason or another, had been unable in their Earthly existence to obtain a proper Catholic burial. But, the Azalea's proprietor, Mr. Goodman Morgan, insures that all his clients have a place to rest, however humble that resting place may be.

Belle enters through the kitchen door. She hangs up her purse, readjusts the back of her wig, and commences to measure coffee grinds into the several coffee pots used for the upcoming all-night Rosary and wakes.

Goodman, Belle's employer, is a portly widower of sixty-plus, with a wry smile. When he enters, he is putting the finishing touches on a corpse. He notices her slightly late arrival, but makes light of it.

"Morning, chèr. I never say 'you're late' at a funeral parlor." He laughs at his attempt to cajole Belle out of her anxious state, but she is embarrassed to have had her rhythm thrown askew by Mr. Thibodeaux.

"I am late, Goodman. Good Lord, I'm so sorry. My grandson, Trent, missed his bus today. It's the first time he's *ever* done that."

"There's a first time for everything. That's what I always say to my 'guests,'" a lilting Goodman chirps back, another failed attempt at funeral parlor jocularity.

Belle's concern for Trent overrides Goodman's attempts to make pleasantries. "This *was* the first time Trent missed the bus and it will be the last, I will assure you that," she says.

"Well, Ms. Belle, let's not fret over what is behind us now. We got us two viewings today. One's a fisherman, Teo Marshall. He's all set up in Parlor Two, 'cept for the accoutrements for his coffin. His wife's bringing 'em. Got caught in a shrimp net, I heard. Poor fella. Twenty-six. Probably gonna' be an all-nighter the way those shrimpers send a man off to the Almighty."

Goodman accidentally drops beige foundation on this corpse's face and suit. "Oh, mon Dieu! Ms. Belle, can you help me out with this mess?"

Belle stops preparing the coffee, comes over to help Goodman. "I used to do some Mary Kay. Oh, my stars! Is that Mr. La Reeve? We can fix his face, but his daughter's going to get after you about the spill on that suit jacket."

"You know him?"

"Why, surely, I did. When his wife died, Trent and I would go and visit. He loved Trent. In his way, he loved me, too. Oh, we had fun. And he just loooved my gumbo. And he was a good dancer."

"Just like I do." Goodman gives her a sweet smile, hoping she'll read the gentlemanly intention behind it. "...love your gumbo, Ms. Belle."

"You like my gumbo, Goodman?"

"Yes'm, I like to dance, too."

"Oh, it's been awhile for me, dancing. I can tell you that."

"I'll bet you're a wonderful dancer. And you are the best coffee lady to ever grace the Azalea Funeral Home, Ms. Belle."

"Why, Goodman, that's so nice of you to say. It's really God's grace to be appreciated. Now, help me get this jacket off of Mr. La Reeve."

Goodman hoists Mr. La Reeve's body up while Belle shimmies off his jacket, Mr. La Reeve's arms already stiff with rigor mortis.

"Oh, for goodness sake, they do set up fast, don't they, Goodman?" Belle pushes down on the sleeves at Mr. La Reeve's wrists and tucks Mr. La Reeve's starched white shirt into his waist. "There you go, Lawrence," she says sweetly. "Now, Goodman, just set him down. He'll be alright."

Her kindness towards Mr. La Reeve is noted by Goodman who can't help but to remark at her care for detail. "Ms. Belle, you are a divine angel come to my abode. I am humbled by your gentle and steadfast care for the deceased."

"Now, Goodman. You go on. I just pray that when it's my time someone will treat me with similar restraint and dignity."

The phone rings. "Azalea Funeral Home, Parlor to Paradise. Goodman Morgan speaking."

"Mr. Morgan, this is Edwin Minor, Shareen La Reeve's husband. I'm just calling to let you know that Shareen is on her way over there to finalize everything because her favorite organist, Mr. Herbert Arsenault, isn't coming out in the storm and she's worried that it will have a negligent appearance on the service."

Goodman signals to Belle about the make-up for Mr. La Reeve's face. "Thank you, Mr. Minor. We'll look forward to seeing her directly, then. I shall obtain the services of another organist."

6 Shareen La Reeve

Shareen La Reeve bursts through the front door of the Azalea Funeral Home. She's a forty-something, overweight, bleached blonde white woman with black hair roots who wears too much mascara and a hot pink lipstick that clashes not only with her bronze contour blush, applied like butane jets on fire along her cheekbones, but which also make her chiclet teeth stand out like garish neon Tic-Tacs in Times Square. You'd never guess she'd used the insurance money to get those teeth fixed after her father's terrible car accident out on the Cane Highway by Spanish Lake, the night Frederick La Grange, who lost to Herbie La Salle in a game of pool, had to (as penance for said loss) drive his brand new truck a hundred miles an hour between Broussard and New Iberia. Unfortunately, Frederick could not keep control of the vehicle and he clipped Lawrence La Reeve's prized Buick Electra 225, causing it to flip over twice and leave it and poor Lawrence La Reeve teetering upside-down and partly submerged on the deeper edge of Spanish Lake. Lawrence somehow managed to get out of the car and when he surfaced, a frantic group of rubberneckers were there to fish him out of the water.

The horror of her father's brush with death understandably drove Shareen to Jesus and now, she's a born-again Christian. She wears dangling crucifix earrings and a gold chain with the word S-A-V-E-D on it and, this afternoon, she sports a rayon navy blue suit with a synthetic Jacqueline Smith floral blouse from K-Mart that would make this Charlie's Angel shudder. Shareen balances precariously in her cork-soled wedgies, followed doggedly by Winston, her disdainful zaftig seventeen-year-old son, dressed too preppie for the occasion, yet whose soft features bespeak a gentle soul, troubled only by the unlucky fortune of being the only child of Shareen La Reeve, real estate saleswoman, and Edwin Minor, tax collector.

"Yoo hoo! Anybody here?" Shareen calls out as she crosses the threshold.

Belle and Goodman, still in the back room, cleaning up Mr. La Reeve, Shareen's father, shudder when they hear her come through the front door.

"Goodman, you go out there and talk to her. I'll take care of Mr. La Reeve's make-up and get the stain off his jacket. I don't want her seeing me. She'd likely strap him to the top of her station wagon and take the poor darling out to another parlor in a different town. And the weather's coming up."

Goodman straightens his own jacket and heads out to the front hallway. "Miss La Reeve..."

Belle pulls her Mary Kay supplies out of her purse. She applies a sponge foundation on Mr. La Reeve's face over the beige blotch, adds bronzer blush with powder, *no time for high-lighter,* mascara on the eyebrows, parts his hair, combs it to one side, gives him a little lip color and blots it quickly.

"Lawrence, you know," Belle whispers to the corpse, "I could make you look really awful on account of the way you broke up with me." Mr. La Reeve doesn't respond, of course. "But, oh, I did love you so, Lawrence. So, I'm going to make you look mighty fine for the Maker. For some time, you were good to my little children, Celestine and Emil, and that guarantees you a holy place in Heaven. I am sure of that. And, I'll say some Rosaries for you tonight when I leave work." She dabs a touch of pink on his cheeks and steps back to admire her work. "I don't normally do this,

Lawrence, but I'll share a little bit of my talc on account of that it's going to be a wet night and I don't want your make-up dripping in this heat."

Out in the hallway, Goodman greets Shareen warmly. "Ms. La Reeve, you are a faithful and dutiful daughter making sure you father is perfectly appointed for Heaven. Rest assured, my dear, that all will be perfect."

She looks past him. "Where's my daddy?"

"He's in the final preparation process."

"Can I see him?"

"No. No. Not at the moment. He's indisposed."

"Dead is about as indisposed as my daddy's ever been to date, Mr. Morgan, Goodman, whatever...." She tries to side-step him. He blocks her. "Can I see him? I wanna see him, *now!*"

"My name is Goodman Morgan. Mr. Morgan, chèr. You can call me anything except late for dinner." He chuckles, buying time for Belle to finish Mr. La Reeve's make-up job.

Shareen's not buying the delay tactic. "What part of 'I wanna see my Daddy, now' do you not understand? You hiding somethin' back there, Mr. Morgan?"

"Nothing. No. Nothing. Not a thing. We're... I'm just fixing his jacket and make-up for the viewing this afternoon. It takes time to do it right. And, we're...I'm awfully busy, trying to get things ready. Your father's service is coming up shortly. Father Gaudet is on his way."

Goodman opens the front door, an invitation for Shareen La Reeve to leave. A wind bustles in. "What? Is that rain already?"

With Winston in tow, Shareen pivots past Goodman and clomps loudly, straight to the back room. Goodman puts his hand on her shoulder to stop her, hoping that Belle's finished her handiwork, and says in a loud voice, "Does your family need some extra hurricane lamps, Ms. La Reeve?"

Shareen looks at his big hand on her shoulder and glares up at him. "You will take your hand off my shoulder, Mr. Morgan." Embarrassed by his mother, Winston looks away. He's more interested in the wallpaper than standing by as his mother rips through yet one more victim of her unpleasant temperament.

Goodman lets go. Shareen pushes through the curtain to the back room. Coffee percolates on the side bar. The corpse of Mr. La Reeve lies in its coffin, sans jacket. Belle is no where to be seen.

Goodman follows in quick pursuit, relieved to see that Belle is not there. Shareen peers over at the corpse, her father. "He looks good. Still fixing his jacket, then?"

"Yes, Ms. La Reeve. I'm about to press it now."

"His hair looks different. But, it's good enough. I'll be back. Rain's comin' up and Winston's got to put the boards on the windows before we come back. Come on, Winston."

Shareen passes by a closet on her way out front. Belle holds her breath and peers from it as Shareen and Winston pass by the door and head out.

Celestine stands inside the closet with Belle. "Nice job, Mama. But, he parted his hair on the right side."

"Oh, my stars, Celestine. You're right! I'll go fix that straight away."

7 School on a Hurricane Day

Beau sits in his homeroom at St. Francis of Assisi High School, across from his best friend, Reginald Robeson Washington, named after Paul Robeson, the great African-American football player and opera singer. Robeson's gift for song transmuted into Reginald, but the athleticism did not.

Reginald is not a handsome boy. However, he is quite striking, with eyes that are deep pools of burnt sienna and a gap—front and center—in his bright white teeth. Just as thin as Beau, Reginald's hair is shortly shorn and perfectly combed. He smells of a mix of "Cool Water" by Davidoff and Nivea skin cream which he uses so that his coal black complexion will not appear ashy.

Fast friends since they were in fifth grade, Beau and Reginald are both excellent students and chivalrous boys. When they were both able to produce fake doctor's excuses to get out of gym class, they would convene in study hall and look up Renaissance architecture, oooohing and aaaahing in disbelief over the pictures of Italy's great cathedrals and gracious ruins. It's never been spoken between them, but they both secretly wish to find themselves someday, somewhere beyond the swampy dreck of the Bayou, something that mostly never happens to students of St. Francis of Assisi High School. This place is its own destiny and few are able to venture beyond it.

Jackson and Lenden, one wearing a N'Oleans Saints t-shirt, jeans and Nikes, and the other wearing a "Ragin' Cajun" t-shirt, jeans and work boots have been shaving since they were twelve. With clear complexions, masculine hair on their chests, hairy arms, these boys will surely end up working at the McIlhenny's company town, if they are lucky. Otherwise, it will be to the salt mines out on Avery Island or the roustabouts off-shore with BP or Texaco. And that will be their livelihood and their lives.

Though Beau and Reginald both have to feign stupidity as a social strategy in school, they have their sights set on horizons far beyond the wildest dreams of most Bayou boys. But, the path from here to anywhere beyond New Iberia is fraught with boggy swamps, potholes, and other obstacles, the least of which are the bullies. To survive, Beau, who has one foot in the

Cajun French culture of illiteracy and another in the erudite offerings of the scholarship of the Humanities, speaks Patois to be understood. Comment m'oui 'e? as opposed to Comment ça va? And for Reginald, his one foot in the Humanities is trumped by the fact that he's Black. So, he speaks Ebonics to get by.

The homeroom teacher, Miss Dupuis, a petite woman with bird glasses sporting rhinestones on their wing-tips, passes out the graded essays to the class. She congratulates Beau and Reginald on their excellent work. "A's again, gentlemen." Beau and Reginald smile a knowing smile to one another, a look that says, one little step further towards the goal of escaping New Iberia. They, of course, avoid looking at their classmates. "Good luck at the debate tournament!" Miss Dupuis chirps and gives them both twinkly smiles, proud of these two diligent students who won the State championship in men's debate at the National American Catholic League Forensic Tournament in Houston, satisfied that they took seriously her lunchtime Scrabble Club. "You know, when you work at Scrabble, your vocabulary just exponentially expands," she says to them, delighting in their accomplishments as her own, but also as an admonition and announcement to the class.

The loudspeaker on the wall by the classroom door crackles. A man clears his throat on the other end, readying for an official announcement which he barks at a military clip: "This is Principal Sonier. Hurricane Rita's turned from the West Florida coast towards Louisiana. We'll be letting school out early. The busses are on their way to pick you up. We have called your parents. If you are seeking shelter here, please let your teacher know...."

At about this moment, in response to the announcement, Reginald and Beau break into perfect two-part syncopated harmony, singing "The Storm is Passing Over." Miming the moves and providing a sound track to the principal as he speaks. "... Your parents will bring your sleeping bag and meet you here. The secretaries and the bus drivers are calling your families right now. If you need to be dropped off on higher ground, all that will be taken care of."

Hamming it up, Miss Dupuis chimes in, "Hallelu!!!" She does a little shimmy and though she receives undeserved smirks from Jackson, Lenden, and the others, she is most appreciated by Beau and Reginald which is all she really cares about, feeding herself on their positive response to her efforts to try to teach anything to any of these utterly dispassionate high school students.

Beau waits for the announcement to be over. Then, looking out at the blustering air, he tells Miss Dupuis, "I need to go check on my brother."

"You may proceed, Beau. And Beau, are you and your brother going to be seeking shelter at school tonight?"

Beau stops by the doorway to answer her, wishing she hadn't asked, "Probably so." The other students snicker because everybody knows that only the poor require shelter at the school.

"You're excused, Beau. But, remember, we're starting at the British expulsion tomorrow."

"Done. And done, Miss Dupuis. The British expulsion of the Acadians from Nova Scotia in 1710 to just before the Cherokee 'Trail of Tears' in 1838. I know it in my bones. I've read ahead. But, I'll read it again. I promise." He flashes her a big smile and tosses his head back, a gesture of dignity and a fuck you to Jackson,

Lenden, and the others who dared to snicker. He *will* show them, in due course. Before he heads out, he turns to Reginald, "Take care, Brother Reginald." Reginald looks up from his book, gives Beau the thumbs up and flashes his wide gap-toothed grin. Their communication, their little jokes, and, most particularly, their joie de vivre is lost on the other students. With back straight and head high, Beau saunters out of the classroom with more than a tad of dramatic flair. Reginald leans back in his chair a moment, taking stock of the cast of characters in the room. He catches Miss Dupuis' eye, as if to acknowledge the sad reality of the situation, "Straight from Central Casting. Isn't that right, Miss Dupuis?"

In the secretary's office, Beau asks to use the phone to call Mawmaw Belle. "I beg your pardon and excuse me for interrupting your excellent work here in running this school, Mrs. Louviere. Oh, that is an exquisite cameo, Mrs. Louviere. But, it is of utmost importance that I find transportation arrangements for my brother."

Mrs. Louviere, a fixture at St. Francis of Assisi High, welcomes Beau into the front office. "How's t'Trent, chèr?"

"Forever happy and thank you for asking. Mmmm...and I do love that scarf your cameo is holding up. That red is a perfect match for your green eyes." Mrs. Louviere loves the attention and they've been through this routine about Trent before with other storms. "You go right ahead," she gestures to the phone. Beau dials Mawmaw Belle first.

Goodman answers, "Azalea Funeral Home, Parlor to Paradise, where flights of angels sing thee to thy rest."

"Good afternoon, Mr. Morgan. It's Beau Landry. May I please speak to my grandmother? School's letting out early."

"You need a ride, right, son?"

"Well, no, sir. I can get one on the bus with Trent."

"Wait!" Goodman says, "I'll do you one better. I'll swing by with the hearse, Beau. Those classmates of yours'll love seeing you boys go off in it." He pauses, listening to the non-response on the other end of the phone. "That's a funeral joke, son."

Now, Beau guffaws. "I get it. And I do love grand exits, Mr. Morgan. Can Reginald ride with us?"

"Why, of course. His mother's working the La Reeve party tonight, anyhow. You and Reginald wait with Trent in the parking lot for me. I'll be leaving directly."

Beau is delighted and relieved to be getting a ride. "Okay, Mr. Morgan. Thank you. I'll get Reginald and we'll walk directly to Trent's school. You know it, right? Archangel Acres." He hangs up.

Mrs. Louviere asks, "All taken care of, Beau? You boys stayin' here tonight, then?"

"Yes, Mrs. Louviere, all taken care of. Thanks ever so. And, no Ma'am, we'll be with my family."

Back at Azalea, Goodman puts on his jacket and grabs his umbrella.

"Ms. Belle, I'm going out for more water. While I'm out, I'll just swing by and pick up Trent, Beau and Reginald."

"Oh, Goodman, Trent will love that, but you shouldn't trouble yourself. The bus can bring them."

But Goodman protests, "After what you told me about Trent's bus driver this morning? No. He'll be safer with me. Let's just get them back here before the storm hits. And, your granddaughter?"

"Janet's mom picks up Felicia and Janet. She'll want to be with her friends anyhow. She always rides with the Labits and they'll drop her off. By the time she gets here, she'll be hungry. It'll give me a little more time to prepare. Now, I've got to go set up Parlor One for Mr. La Reeve's Rosary."

Beau gets Reginald and the two hightail it over to the Archangel Acres Middle School where Trent waits with the other Special-Ed students and their teacher and where the school janitors are quickly putting boards up on the windows.

When Goodman arrives in his Lincoln Continental hearse, he leans out the window and calls out to Beau, Trent, and Reginald. "Hot Rod to Heaven. Who wants a ride?"

Beau helps Trent with his bag. "Come on, Trent. Mr. Morgan's taking us to Mawmaw. He's come to fetch us from the storm. Get you in." Then, Beau leans out the side window and says to the waiting students, "Don't be scared when Mr. Goodman honks the horn. Just hold your ears, like this." He shows them how.

Goodman puts his hand over Trent's shoulder, "Hey, t'Trent. Good day at school, chèr?"

"I not miss school. Tank you bery much, please."

"But he almost missed the bus this morning, Mr. Morgan." Beau chimes in.

"I not miss bus, Beau."

"Touché, Trent. You're correct. You did not miss the bus. The bus missed you."

Goodman pats Trent on the shoulder. "Well, Gentlemen, let's go get us some more water and take you back to your Mawmaw." He guns the hearse engine, toots the horn for the kids, waves, and heads out, calling to the gentlemen in the car "Garçons, laissez les bon temps rouler!"

Beau and Reginald, ever the soul-sister merry pranksters, sing "It's a Highway to Heaven."

It's a highway to Heaven
None can walk up there
But the pure in heart
It's a highway to Heaven
I am walking up the King's highway...
Hallelujah! Amen!

8 Father Gaudet

When the boys enter with Goodman, Belle hugs and kisses them all, embracing them with all her heart.

"Bonjour, chèrs. You're back! Reginald, welcome. Your mother and grandmother are in the kitchen. Beau, here's Trent's funeral tie. Can you do the honors? I'll give you all sandwiches when you're dressed for the guests. There are two parties tonight. Have you heard from Felicia?"

"No, Mawmaw. Not a word." Beau helps Trent on with his tie.

Belle, still fretting about Shareen La Reeve, "Goodman, what are we going to do? I don't think Shareen would like for me to be near her father's Rosary!"

"You nevermind her, I'll do what I always do, Ms. Belle. I'll let my trusted staff do their jobs."

With the black tie on, Trent now stands at the ready by the front door. Father Gaudet, seventy-five, and all of about five foot six or seven, dressed in his priest robes, enters.

Trent points to the room where Mr. La Reeve's coffin now rests. "The body is over here. Please. Tank you bery much."

Father Gaudet smiles at Trent, "Hey, chèr, you've got a job! And, what's that around your neck, t'Trent?"

Proudly, Trent leans forward to show him. "That be my medals." Celestine looks on with pride, too.

"You doin' good, chèr. You doin' good."

"My Mama say hi," Trent tells him. "She smile when you come."

Father Gaudet pats him on the shoulder. "Pauvre garçon, mon Dieu." He leaves Trent behind at the door and heads into Parlor One. Celestine stands beside Trent and pats his shoulder, too. "That was good, Trent. It will help affirm his faith in the Hereafter."

In the parlor, Father Gaudet sets up the Holy Water. Goodman enters. "Good afternoon, Father."

"Ah, Mr. Morgan, how you be?"

"Comme ci, comme ça, thank you. Rita's comin', Father. Let's pray it's not another Katrina," Goodman looks out the window.

But, Father Gaudet is not concerned. He's not planning on going back out into the rain, "Yes, but, the

Rosary will last all night. Everyone will be safe here. They always are, Mr. Morgan."

Goodman raises the coffin cover. "The family wants the wake 'open coffin.' The private showing for the family will be from four to five. The rest of the guests will arrive around five o'clock."

Father Gaudet checks his watch. "They're gonna' want to eat before the Rosary, so we can begin it at six."

"Yessir. And Mrs. Ursula Washington will be serving the La Reeve party."

Father crosses himself, "God bless her for coming out in this weather."

"It's a livin', Father," Goodman jabs out his elbow, with a sly smile, indicating it's a joke. But, Father Gaudet misses it. Disappointed, Goodman leaves to attend to the next thing, leaving the Father to go through his pre-Rosary ritual.

Father Gaudet anoints his fingers with the Holy Water. He makes the sign of the cross over Mr. La Reeve's body: the forehead, the mouth, the heart. He blesses the rosary Mr. La Reeve will hold in his hands and sets it into Mr. La Reeve's grasp. He blesses the Crucifix that is on the inner lid of the coffin. He kneels down, pulls out a flask from his robe, takes a swig of Bourbon, and prays by the coffin.

"Blessed be, Father. I ask for your mercy to receive Mr. Lawrence La Reeve into your Heavenly realm. Holy Spirit guide my tongue." As he pours his drink, "If Jesus drank wine to guide his words, guide mine, Lord, so I don't slur." He raises his flask. "Amen. Amen, Chèr."

Shareen, Edwin, and Winston arrive.

In her usual condescending tone, she scoffs that Trent is the welcoming committee. "Oh, hello, Trent." She doesn't like to associate with anyone with a mental affliction, lest it infect her or her son. "Take my jacket, Edwin." He dutifully helps her off with it and holds it over his arm. She hands her faux leather alligator purse to him while she pulls down on her too-tight black spandex dress. Winston looks down the hallway for Beau, but he's not in view.

Oblivious to her scorn, Trent dutifully points to Parlor One, "The body is over here. Please. Tank you bery much." Edwin pivots to head into the room, but Shareen pulls him back. "What's your rush, Edwin?"

Well, the rush is that Edwin, being all of three hundred and fifty pounds wants to find a seat. And, not only that, he wants to insure that he gets the most comfortable chair in Parlor One, knowing this will be a long night of praying and greeting friends and family of a father-in-law who never could understand what his daughter saw in him—these not-so-subtle injustices never quite having resolved in his heart, even with the passing of the offending party.

Shareen clasps Edwin's fleshy forearm to keep him from moving, her nails like a bear trap clamping his radius and ulna so tightly, he can feel bone pressing against bone. "Now, what's that around your neck, Trent?" she says, not really wanting to engage him, but awkwardly extending an uncustomary (for her) modicum of courtesy to the boy.

Proudly leaning forward, as he did for Father Gaudet, Trent shows Shareen, "That be my medals."

Edwin smiles and leans in to look at them. "Trent, you must be so proud."

"Hush-up, Edwin," Shareen sneers when she sees Trent's Special Olympics medals, "Looks like something from Mardi Gras." Edwin obediently and awkwardly slumps into submission. He smiles weakly at Trent, but says nothing.

Belle peers through the curtain. *Okay, Shareen La Reeve, you uneducated little witch, now you've overstepped it. I am a patient woman, but you are not going to speak to my Trent like that.* She hands Beau a coffee pot and tray with cups, spoons, and sugar. "Beau, you go out there with this and just make sure Shareen La Reeve doesn't upset Trent."

"I'm all prepared to use the duck tape, Mawmaw!" Belle laughs, grateful to have a comrade-in-arms in her historical battle with Shareen La Reeve.

"And don't you spill that tray of coffee on her...her... ill-fitting dress, either. You go on, now. Go on. Offer some coffee to her family. Maybe you could get Father Gaudet to share some of his 'holy water' with that poor benighted husband of hers while I'm fixing the men's coffee."

Beau steps out from between the hanging curtain over the kitchen door. Shareen looks to Beau.

"Why Beau, you look good, considering..."

"You're looking well, yourself, Ms. Shareen, considering... And, I'm so sorry to see your dear father in this state. My grandmother loved him so."

"We parked out back by your mama's grave, Beau. Shame that she couldn't rest in a Christian cemetery," Shareen snips back at him. Belle hears that. *Oooh, don't push me into a fight, Shareen La Reeve.* Shareen has no scruples when it comes to figuring out ways to push the buttons of anyone who has any connection to Belle Boudreaux.

~ ~ ~

Meanwhile, miles away, Popo Cole builds something that looks like a make-shift tree-house, only the shape of it resembles a coffin-like container -- solid, wooden, and up in a tree, at least six feet above the ground, above the water line.

~ ~ ~

Beau stands straight and tall, confident that his education, even in high school, surpasses Shareen's eighth grade C-minus graduation certificate. "And Mr. La Reeve will be right across the street, n'est-ce pas?"

"My daddy's got the best spot in the new mausoleum. He's six feet up, in case of floodin'. I spared no expense on having things done right for Daddy. And thank goodness we got your Mawmaw's claws off'a him, so I can afford this whole..."

Beau interrupts her, "I'm sure that my grandmother and the Azalea Funeral Home will make sure that all of your needs are met." He sniffs the air. "Oh, Winston. My, my... Hugo Boss?"

Winston perks up. "Yes."

"Hmmm," Beau looks him up and down. "Maison Blanc?"

Winston replies, "Robicheaux's."

Beau winks at him, "Hmm. They're moving up."

Winston blushes, "Indeed, they are."

The gay-code between them is lost on Shareen. She's somehow missed the obvious fact of Winston's effeminate nature.

Beau offers Shareen some coffee, "Black?" He pours it. To Winston, he says, "Got everything boarded up for your Mama?"

"Yes" is all Winston can muster.

By now, Beau has become overtly flirtatious, partly to annoy Shareen, "Oh, how we labor, Winston!" But, she isn't paying attention.

Winston looks at his own suit and with a coy smile, "But, at least, we're dressed well."

"I need some sugar with that, Beau," Shareen barks.

"Oh, well, you'll have to add that yourself, Shareen. Here you go. I have a whole bowl of it for you." He holds out the tray with the sugar on it. She takes four cubes. While regarding her body stuffed into her dress, Beau quips, "To your health, Shareen."

"Beau, has my maid arrived? I'm sure my guests will be hungry."

"Oh, yes, Shareen, Mrs. Washington is already in the kitchen."

Shareen turns on her heels and beelines for the kitchen. Edwin and Winston head to Parlor One, Edwin still carrying Shareen's faux alligator purse.

9 The Azalea Kitchen and Ursula Washington

Mrs. Ursula Washington, a sturdy Black woman in her early forties, wears a white maid's apron over her navy blue skirt and white blouse, her hair, straight and pressed with a hot comb earlier in the day, is holding up even as this is her second shift today and she'll be cooking all night. She stirs a pot of Catfish Sauce Piquant. Miss Ursula's face gleams and she, too, has a space between her teeth, just like Reginald. Her sixty-year-old mother, Odetta, sits at the kitchen table, folding napkins.

Odetta is a small, sinewy black women with kind eyes. She has dark, arthritic hands from picking cotton, sugar cane, and peppers. Reginald's father is in the penitentiary for wrongly correcting Sheriff Raleigh and not knowing his place like a good Black man should. Odetta's husband's arm was ripped off on a cotton gin. They were able to sew it back on, but he died shortly thereafter. The infection from the wound-sewing killed him, leaving Reginald as the man of the house at a tender age, just like Beau.

Shareen enters like a drill sergeant, "Mrs. Washington, I need *you*, not your family."

Ursula, stifling her honest reaction, answers as politely as any domestic servant must. "They're having across the Bayou to evacuate, Mrs. La Reeve. I had to bring them with me."

"Well, then, your mother can pass out towels to my guests in the bathroom and your son can help with coats and umbrellas."

Hearing this, Goodman enters the back end of the conversation, "No. No. No. No, Ms. La Reeve. The coats and umbrellas have been taken care of. Reginald's got homework to do."

"He's gotta learn how to make a livin', Mr. Morgan. I'm giving him an opportunity. Can't you see that?"

Thirty seconds of Shareen is about all the patience Odetta's able to give her. "He's got homework. Didn't you hear? He makes straight A's. He's going to college," she proudly sets Shareen straight.

Ursula gives her mother a look: *Mama, no!*

But Goodman agrees with Odetta. "He'll be running for judge of New Iberia before you know it."

"Not in this parish." Shareen lifts an eyebrow at them all and pivots out.

Odetta turns to her daughter, "Lotta' pressure on those little biddy shoes, don't you know?"

"Oh, Mama, please."

Odetta looks up to the ceiling, "Oh, Lord, help me. Give me your strength so that I may hold my tongue. And is this the woman I raised to stand up for herself?"

Everyone laughs.

Ursula turns away from the stove, "Forgive me for what I'm thinkin'."

Reginald, who's been a silent observer of this ugly exchange, "Forgive us for what we all thinkin'."

They laugh heartily. Goodman, too.

Shareen now spies Belle and clomps loudly through the front hallway towards her.

The front door opens. Felicia stands there like a wet cat, her hair all wilted, the sugar cubes melted and sticky on the drooping satin ribbons.

Beau dramatically gasps, "What happened to your sugar cubes?"

Felicia froths, "What happened to your face?"

Shareen shrieks at Belle, "Are you working or are you running a babysittin' service, here?" She stomps off to check on Edwin who has commiserated with Father Gaudet over the sad occasion by imbibing in some of the Father's special holy water.

"Already, Edwin! I can smell liquor on your breath. Give me the flask." She rips open his jacket, but nothing is there.

Edwin pats his body. "Honey, bunny. I ain't got no flask. Maybe it's the fermentation from the cheese sandwich I ate at lunch." He burps on cue and she purses her lips so tightly she might have put a permanent pucker in her already seriously compromised mug.

Shareen looks to Father Gaudet for help. But he feigns to be deep in prayer, preparing himself for the evening's solemnity.

"Well, I have guests to greet!" Shareen stomps out.

Belle sucks it up when Shareen marches by them again. To Beau and Felicia, "Y'all can't take the fight outside cause it's raining. So, y'all best be civil. Go in the back room." She puts on her best professional smile and turns back to Shareen, "It's looking like it's going to be a long night, eh, Shareen?"

Felicia fingers her hair, sticky from the matted sugar. "Do you have a hair dryer here?"

"No, Darlin'. But, there's a fan in the Utility Room."

"Nevermind."

"If you got that short and sassy haircut like Natalie Portman, I wanted you to get, I wouldn't have to worry about rolling your hair all the time. And you wouldn't have to worry about a biddie rainfall."

Them's fighin' words for Felicia, "No, I'll let Beau get the Natalie Portman haircut. And this ain't no biddie rainfall."

Belle ushers her towards the back, "Go in the back, dry off, and start your homework. I'll bring you a chicken salad sandwich."

"Funeral food!"

"Felicia Marie!"

Beau chimes in, "But the crusts are cut off!"

Felicia's like a dog on a leash, resisting a walk. "I'm not going back there if there are dead bodies."

"No, Sugar," Belle assures her, "all the bodies are on display. The room is empty."

"It smells in there."

"I can't smell it."

"You can't smell nothin' with that ridiculous-smelling perfume," Felicia lobs it back at her grandmother.

While this is going on, Beau opens Belle's purse and pulls out a handkerchief, sprays it with perfume.

Exasperated with her granddaughter, "Just go to the sun porch in back, then. It's all boarded up for the hurricane."

"I'm not going there. Mama's buried back by that sun porch."

Beau hands the perfumed handkerchief to Felicia and turns her shoulders away from where they are standing by the front door. "May your journey to the porch be fragrant and sweet."

There is a crash from the wind.

Goodman comes by, carrying a tray of finger food for Parlor One. "The weatherman says it's fifty miles south of Morgan City now."

Belle regains her compassion for Felicia, "I'm sorry, honey. There's no other place for you to be right now."

But, Felicia will not go either to the back room or the sun porch. She counters with, "What about the kitchen?"

Goodman asserts his authority, "Belle, it's alright. She's probably scared. Let her stay in the kitchen with the rest of us."

"Thank you, Mr. Morgan. Now, be good, Felicia. I'm still working."

"You're always working."

"Felicia, your brother and I work to pay the bills, to put clothes on your back, and food in your stomach. I raised your mother, Celestine, and your Uncle Emil, and now I'm raising you. That's just life."

Felicia gives Belle a snotty look. Belle reaches out to hug her. But, Felicia stiffens and plops the handkerchief back into Belle's open palm.

Lightning flashes. A clap of thunder. The door blows open as more La Reeve guests arrive.

Trent points, "The body is over here. Tank you bery much, please."

Beau pulls the rosaries from their box. "I'll be checkin' the rosaries in Parlor One, Mawmaw."

Back in the kitchen, Goodman brings in a transistor radio. He adjusts the frequency.

The radio announces: *Hurricane Tracker. Rita's moving westward at a speed of 120 miles per hour. Anticipate landfall in about two hours.*

Goodman takes Belle aside. "Ms. Belle, I wanted to say how sorry I am that you're having to work for the La Reeve party."

"Oh, I'm a lucky woman, Goodman. I can see now how much the good Lord protected me from that daughter of his."

Felicia, as if snapping to, looks at Belle, astonished. "His daughter?"

Goodman sets the radio on the shelf. "I think we best check in with the tracker as much as we can."

In an attempt to deflect where she thinks this conversation is headed, Belle adds, "Felicia, some people work themselves into a snit over money. That's all I'm saying."

"Well," Goodman smiles at Belle, "Mr. La Reeve had good taste in women."

Felicia, chewing her sandwich, "What women?"

Belle admonishes her, "It's really none of your concern, Felicia. Eat your sandwich."

"Mawmaw, everybody knows you went out with that dead guy."

10 Boudreaux Kitchen in the Long Lost Past

Young Belle, twenty-six, wearing a white cotton dress with blue morning glories, irons while young Mr. La Reeve, about forty-five, who looks strikingly like Winston (but with a much trimmer physique), his straight hair parted on the side and slicked back with Royal Crown pomade, sits at Belle's kitchen table. He says to her, "Belle, chèr, why you ironing the pillow cases?"

"Nothing's good enough for you, Boo." She smiles with a flirtatious gleam in her eyes.

Young Celestine, age five, sitting with her little brother, Emil, maybe all of three years old, in front of the TV in another room, chews nervously on her hair while watching cartoon characters clobber one another in mirthful violence. Emil plays with a toy truck, occasionally distracted by the screams on the screen. Belle keeps an eye on her little daughter and son through the door.

Young Mr. La Reeve leans back in his chair, "Belle, chèr, how long we been going out together now?"

"About eight months, Lawrence."

"Oh, yes, it's been so fine. You are a fine woman, Ms. Belle. I love you so much."

Belle sets the iron on its holder and goes over to sit on the lap of young Lawrence La Reeve, "And, I love you, too, Lawrence. I love you ten times more than I ever loved my children's father."

The phone rings. Belle picks it up. "Hello?" It's Shareen, about sixteen, demanding, "Is my daddy over there? Let me speak to him."

Belle holds the phone out, "It's your daughter." She goes back to her ironing.

Young Mr. La Reeve takes the phone. "What's going on, Shareen? Sure, honey, you can come over. Belle's got some gumbo on." He hangs up.

Young Mr. La Reeve looks long at Belle and says, "Belle, put that iron down. I want to ask you somethin' and I'm serious."

"Lawrence, you're never serious."

"I'm as serious as a heart attack. Chèr, let's get married."

"What about your daughter?"

"Oh, nevermind her. I have my own life to live."

"But, Lawrence, she calls on you every fifteen minutes every time you're over here. She won't leave us alone for two seconds. How do you think she's going to be about us getting married?"

Young Mr. La Reeve wraps his arms around Belle, reassuringly, "Belle, I said it's my life. Now, how about Sunday, Baby? In the park. Under the willow tree. What say you? You sit there. Let me propose proper." Young Mr. La Reeve gets on his knees.

"Sunday?" Belle's not sure. "That's a little hurried for planning a wedding."

But, La Reeve won't take no for an answer, "I'll bring some fried oysters. You make some black-eyed peas."

She looks at him lovingly. They kiss.

"Oh, Lawrence.... You prefer corn bread or white rice?"

He thinks for a second, "Corn bread."

"And coconut or pineapple cake?"

"Both, chèr."

They kiss again.

"Se promener. Your kids. My kids. And I'll invite Hazel and Bob."

"Lawrence, with my extra job, I don't have time to sew a dress."

Young Mr. La Reeve reaches into his wallet and pulls out a hundred dollar bill. "Go buy yourself a beautiful dress, my bride."

"Why Lawrence, that's too much money!"

"Then, buy you a dress and buy something for Celestine and Emil. Keep the change."

Young Belle throws herself into Young Mr. La Reeve's arms. They kiss again.

He stands up, "I best meet Shareen at the door. And I'll break the news to her when I get home. I'll see my bride in the park on Sunday morning."

"Are you sure about this, Lawrence? I'm worried about Shareen..."

Young Shareen bangs on the door as she let's herself in. "Daddy, you got your dentures in?"

To his daughter, "Mais, Belle's family."

Young Shareen snaps at her father, "You put your teeth in when you eatin' over here. It's not right."

But, Young Mr. La Reeve protests. "I can't believe you gonna' make me put my teeth in, Shareen. I won't be able to taste Belle's gumbo."

"You best come home then, if you cain't eat proper."

Figuring Shareen's arrival might end like this, Belle's been packing up some gumbo for them.. "Here you go. Take it home. Bye-bye, Shareen. Bye, Lawrence."

Young Mr. La Reeve takes his dentures out of his pocket and puts them into his mouth. Belle watches as Lawrence's daughter practically drags him out her kitchen door.

"Sunday, ma Belle." He winks, puts on his hat, and tips it to her one last time. "Sunday, chèr."

I'm surprised she didn't tow him out by his ear. I hope she can be pleasant on Sunday, for a change.

11 The Wedding Picnic

Young Belle sits on a picnic bench, posed in a silk chiffon periwinkle flower tea length dress, her young children, Celestine and Little Emil, by her side.

To prepare for the wedding picnic, she'd gone to Tante Rosalie's and picked every gardenia and every rose in her garden. That Spring, Tante's wild rose bushes were so full. Belle starched and ironed her little children's clothes and laid out her grandmother's chantilly-laced table cloth on the table. She set the most beautiful picnic with flowers around all the plates. And she pinned a little boutonniere on Emil's shirt and made a chain of daisies for Celestine's head.

She sat and waited under that willow tree with her children in their Sunday best. The lilac powder under her arms was dripping with sweat and turning to icing, like the pineapple-coconut icing that was dripping down that cake and onto all the flowers in that hot hot sun. She waited and waited and waited, alone with her children and the beautiful spread of food all laid out, until the sun started to set. And, finally, she implored to God, "Why are you doing this to me?" Tears ran down Belle's face.

Little Celestine, reached up to dry the wetness on her mother's cheeks, "Don't cry, Mama. Mama, don't cry."

Belle gathered up her broken heart and fed the children.

～　～　～

And, telling this story to Goodman, she recalls, "And so, my children had black-eyed peas and pineapple-coconut cake for supper. And I took every dirty plate and put them in the center of my grandmother's table cloth and I carried it to the Bayou and threw it in and I said, "As God is my witness, no man will ever put me through that again."

With tears in his eyes, Goodman puts both hands on Belle's shoulders, wanting to hold her close, but not wanting to be improper in the midst of the funerals about to take place at the Azalea. "The things we do for love, chèr. Très tragique, chèr, non?" he says. He puts his thumb under her chin and lifts her face gently up towards his, smiling his sweet smile. "You are strong, chèr. Beautiful and strong. Ai-je raison?"

"Too strong, sometimes, I think, Goodman. Too strong," she sighs. "The real tragedy is that he broke my heart that day."

"Miss Belle, he didn't deserve you." Goodman releases his physical connection to her.

She looks down the hallway towards Parlor One. "That's the last time I saw Lawrence La Reeve, until today."

"So, it was, chèr. So, it was. We've had our losses, n'est-ce pas? I guess you'd heard that my wife, Patty, drove my Baby off the bridge."

"Your baby!"

12 Goodman's Blue Camero

"Yes, Baby. My twilight blue Camero Z28. '69. A great year for cars as car history goes. I was twenty-five. I was laying on my back, working under Baby when Patty stood in the doorway. She knew how much I loved blue and was wearing a baby blue Doris Day dress that day herself...."

"Goodman? Goodman!" Patty calls out to him.

"I asked her if my dinner was ready. She said, 'Goodman! I think you love that car more than you love me.'"

"Well, Miss Belle, I told Patty not to be silly, that there was no comparison. But, I probably should have been more honest. I did love that car more than just about anything in the world. Patty wasn't even really a close second. I was young and didn't appreciate what it meant to have a woman in my life..." He trails off.

~ ~ ~

"Patty said, 'Really, Goodman?'"

"And I said, 'Really.' But, she issued me a challenge. 'Well, you gonna' let me drive it, then, or not?' she said. And I shuddered, thinking about her behind the wheel of Baby. It was a cold chill that ran through me. Farouchement froid, chèr! Fiercely cold.

"'Not,' I said, 'Patty, there are just some things you don't ask a man to do for.'

"Thankfully, I was under Baby, so Patty couldn't see my face all screwed up at the thought of her even touching the steering wheel of my prized possession. I said to her, 'You can't drive it, Patty. You're not used to a locked steering wheel.'

"She sidled up beside me, leaned down and looked under the car. 'I'd look awfully good drivin' it. Don't you think, Goodman?' she said.

"But I was firm. Well, wouldn't you know, she had fit and slammed the door. I learned that night it's best not to go to bed with your wife angry. The next night, when I was at work and we had two all night funerals, like tonight, it was rainin' cats and dogs. She snuck the keys to Baby and drove out up along the highway. I can imagine she had the radio turned up high. She liked Tammy Wynette songs. He hums: '*There goes my reason for living... There goes the one of my dreams... There goes my only possession... There goes my everything.*'

"She'd been out grocery shopping, I guess. I don't know what she was doing going over the Miracle of Mother Mary Bridge. You know, the one that straddles where Bayou Teche, Bayou La Forche, and the Atchafalaya Basin come together? Probably thought it was a shorter way home as the weather was so bad that evening. But the bridge was washed out. They told me there was a sign saying so. I don't know how Patty missed it. Likely, she was singing at the top of her lungs and feeling mighty feisty that she'd gotten away in Baby, right out from under my nose.

"She ended up driving off the bridge and banged down a cliff on the riverbank. The engine probably cut out. I'm sure she tried to get it going. But, once it had turned off, the steering wheel needed that little extra something to get it unhinged from its locked position and she just didn't have enough experience driving that car to know how to do it.

"Patty drove herself and my mint-condition Camero z28 into the Mississippi River. It took 'em about two weeks to find the car. I got a call here at the Azalea from the state troopers. They told me where to show up to claim her.

"When I got there, a tow-truck and some workmen were hauling Baby from the muddy water. It had drifted two miles down the Mississippi. Patty was no where to be found. There was a two foot rip in the convertible top which Patty must have made with her nail file in an attempt to escape. But, obviously, she didn't make it, either.

"Her body turned up near Avery Island about two weeks after that. The McIlhenny's offered to pay for her funeral arrangements. Lucky for them, Patty was the wife of the owner of the only funeral parlor in New Iberia. Rumor had it, they took it as a tax write-off anyways."

～ ～ ～

Belle pats Goodman's shoulder. "There, there, Goodman. That is a sad story."

"You bet. It took that car forever to dry out and the convertible top had to be completely replaced. But, Baby's back in mint condition now. I keep her in my closed garage." His eyes mist up. "Miss Belle, if you don't mind my asking...?"

"What is it, Goodman?"

"What happened to your husband? Didn't go off the bridge like my Patty Mae."

"Popo Cole? Simplement disparu. He was a wild man, had a calling, it seems. Il est un traiteur. One day, the swamp just called him to her and that was that."

"You were divorced, then?"

"They say, after seven years, if you can't find someone, then he's dead. But, I know he's out there somewhere. But to marry Lawrence, I had to act like Popo Cole was dead. He's alive though, I know it in my bones. But I had to move on, Goodman. I had to go on. Our daughter, Celestine was never buried in a Christian cemetery, though, because I couldn't receive communion on account of not being properly unmarried."

Goodman, incredulous, "Well, that's just stupid, if you ask me. Surely, by now, there would be no problem."

Belle isn't sure. "Celestine, Beau and I did everything we could so Trent could receive communion. But, on account of my situation, it was too late for their mama, when she died."

13 Dat Be Jesus

"It was back, oh, I don't know...Trent was maybe all of twelve years old. He understood a lot, but he just couldn't respond too well. Celestine, Beau and I were all sitting at the kitchen table with Trent. Beau, he must have been eleven, was trying to get Trent to answer the confirmation questions."

~ ~ ~

"Now, Trent," Beau positions himself in front of Trent's gaze to get eye contact, "There are questions that Father Rodriguez asks for confirmation. We're going to do it together. You got that?"

Trent holds onto his Scooby Doo doll and answers, glancing away from Beau towards Scooby. "Yes, please, tank you bery much."

"We're going to keep it simple, Trent. Now, watch."

Beau reaches over to Trent's right hand and places it on his forehead. "Right here, on your forehead is the Father. That is God the Father." Beau moves Trent's hand to his heart. "And here is the Son. The Son, that's Jesus. He is in your heart, Trent. Right here." Beau moves Trent's hand to his left shoulder and then to his right shoulder. "And here, Trent, is the Holy Spirit. Amen. Let's do it again. Father here. Son here. And Holy Spirit here. Amen."

"Amen. Please. Tank you bery much," Trent agrees, rocking.

Beau tries so very hard to explain how it's going to work. "When Father Rodriguez asks you any question, Trent, what do you say?"

"I love Jesus. Tank you bery much please. Father Son Holy Spirit. Amen."

Belle, Celestine, and Beau all laugh.

"Yes, Trent. You got that right. Jesus loves you and you love Jesus. That'll do."

But, Celestine wasn't convinced it would do. "Beau, I don't know if this is going to work."

"Mama, I will be with him."

Belle pipes in, "No matter what, Celestine, we need to let the angel speak. Trent knows no malice. If Father Rodriguez doesn't recognize that, then we need not go to the door of that church anymore. That's all." ...

... "I tried to assure my daughter, Goodman, 'I think Trent's got it, Celestine.' But, she was a worrier, always fretting about something. Beau assured her, too...."

"We're just not going through the front door, Momma. We're using the back door. But, he'll get there! Don't you worry. I'll be with him every step of the way."

Celestine leans on her elbows on the table. "Oh, the hoops we go through." She puts her face in her hands and heaves a long slow sigh.

Belle pats her daughter's arm, "It's in God's hands, Celestine. His will be done."

Celestine decides to test Trent once more. "Trent, honey, I'm going to ask you one question from the Confirmation. You ready?" ....

The next day Trent stands with Beau by the baptismal font. Father Rodriguez asks them the confirmation questions. Celestine, Belle, and Felicia look on.

Trent looks past the Father and says, "In the name of Father Son Holy Spirit Amen. I love Jesus. Tank you bery much please. Amen."

Father Rodriguez does the sign of the cross on Trent and Beau, shakes their hands. Trent heads down the aisle, dragging Scooby Doo and beaming. The church is mostly empty with only a few parishioners in attendance. But, Trent talks to them on his way down the aisle, smiling all the way.

"Dat be Jesus! Dat be Jesus!"

14 Easter Bunny Bingo

Shortly after Trent's confirmation, he woke up early, excited about Easter. "Da Easter Bunny be coming on Jesus mornin'," he told the family at breakfast.

Celestine shot Belle a look of despair. There wasn't going to be an Easter Bunny this year. No money.

Beau said, "Mama, we can explain it to him."

But, Celestine said, "Don't be ridiculous. He's expecting the Easter Bunny and that's that. I'd sell my arm for a bag of candy tonight."

"Y'all sound like a junkie, Momma!" Beau reached out to her, but she was simply in too much despair about it to respond.

"I'm serious, Beau. Look at him. He can't wait for that magic rabbit to show up. And, how am I gonna' pull a rabbit out of my skinny behind? Should we just hide the invisible basket so good that he'll never find it? What a clever rabbit that would be."

Belle chimed in. "That'd be mean. Celestine. You need some rest, honey. Let me take the boys to Bingo. Try to get your mind off tomorrow. All we got is today."

"Yes, take them, Mama. I don't have the energy anyway. I don't even have a nickel for a Bingo card!"

Belle kisses Celestine on the head. "Honey, the Lord is watching over Trent. I know, at least, that to be true. He watches over all his angels."

"I wish I believed that, Maman. I just wish I believed that."

When Felicia went to bed, Belle, Beau, and Trent headed out to Bingo.

As soon as they left, Celestine got up and rifled through a file box, where she found a document she was looking for. She gave it a cursory look and left it on the kitchen table and headed into the bathroom.

～ ～ ～

Belle and her grandchildren enter the church basement meeting room where Bingo is underway and Belle buys three cards for herself, one for Beau, and one for Trent.

The Bingo Caller, Mr. Lloyd Robichaux, dressed in a ruffled red and white striped shirt, a straw hat, his pants held up with suspenders, shows the prizes to the Bingo players.

"Hello! Hello! Come on in! Welcome! Welcome! Come, have a seat. Welcome to Basement Bingo Night, y'all. Welcome! Welcome!"

Belle and Beau usher Trent to a table with three empty seats.

Lloyd Robichaux holds up a rice cooker. "We've got some lovely prizes this evening. Check this out. First prize is a Con Rico rice cooker. Now, that's something that would come in handy in any kitchen. Looky that. It's a lovely thing, isn't it? Next here, these strawberry fig preserves. Hmmm. Now, who made this lovely stuff?"

Shirley Perman, a buttery plump woman who's blouse buttons, pulled tight across her chest, expose her brassiere anyway, raises her hand. "I did!"

Belle, more relaxed than usual, calls across the room, "Oh, yes, Shirley. Tha's good, I'm sure of it. Your reputation as a *fine* cook goes far and wide."

"Why Miss Belle, where on Earth did you hear about my cookin'?"

Laraine LaGrieve looks up from her Bingo card, and calls across to Shirley, "MmmmMmmmm, Shirley, don't ask a question you don't want answered. There's an awful lot of tire tracks out there by your tent!" A knowing laughter erupts from the Bingo crowd. It's all good fun. Everyone knows that Shirley Perman has a steady stream of visitors when she's not in her beauty shop out on Highway 42.

Lloyd Robichaux holds up a seafood platter. "Okay, ladies, keep it down. Keep it down. We got us a free seafood platter from Preagan's and a laundry basket here with Easter candy in it."

Belle nudges Beau, "Hey, Beau, looks like your Mama's not going to have to sell her arm, after all. We're going to win that laundry basket, I just know it. Okay, Trent, now let's all work on one card together."

Mr. Robichaux calls out the first number. "Our first number is Twenty-eight. Two. Eight."

"Well, would you look at that! I got twenty-eight!" Belle exclaims.

Mr. Robichaux picks another number. "Sixty-three. Six. Three."

Beau shouts, "We got it!" He places his number on the Bingo card.

"Seventeen. One. Seven."

Belle shrieks. "Again? Why, I should have bought a lottery ticket. Look at how we're doing!"

"Forty-two. Four. Two."

But they don't have that number. "No. Now, Belle, don't get greedy," she says to herself out loud. "You got three on there, now. That's good."

Belle pulls out her rosary and hand-prays it under the table.

Lloyd Robicheaux calls out, "Nine. That is a Zero Niner."

Other Bingo players put pennies on their Bingo cards.

"Thirty-seven. Three. Seven."

Belle squeals. "Well, will you look at that! I put down all my pieces."

Trent holds his piece—a twelve.

Belle turns to Beau, "I should have let Trent take one of my pieces, Beau. You and I have both played ours, but Trent hasn't played anything. That wasn't fair of us, was it?"

Trent anxiously grips his chip and watches.

"The game's not over, Mawmaw. There are lots of numbers to go."

Dolly Fornier, a middle-aged lady-friend of Belle's, dressed in a crayon pink stretch shirt with a baby blue feather boa and black jeans, comes by to wish everyone a good holiday.

"Happy Easter tomorrow, Belle, Beau, and Brother Trent. Mais, how be you?"

"We're good, Dolly. We're good. I'm just taking a little biddy moment to enjoy my grandchildren. And, how're you?"

"Well, my husband's not doing too good, but I'm still kicking."

"I am so sorry to hear about that, Dolly. I'll pray for him tonight, dear."

"Thank you. Thank you so very much, Belle. That's mighty kind of you."

Lloyd Robichaux calls out. "Twelve. A one and a two."

Trent shouts as loud as he can, "Bingo!!!"

Everyone knows Trent. The room erupts with cheers.

"Come on up here, Trent Landry, and claim your prize from old Lloyd."

With Beau's help, Trent holds their Bingo card and carries it to the front. On the way through the tables, Trent shows off his Special Olympics medals hanging on his neck.

"Congratulations, son."

Trent chooses the Easter Basket, of course.

Belle cries, "It's an Easter miracle!"

"Mawmaw, it's a sign from God. Now, Momma really doesn't have to worry about the Easter Bunny not showing up with a basket of candy."

Belle, Beau, and Trent return home. Just outside the door, when Beau reaches for the door knob, he senses that something's not right.

"Mawmaw...."

"Beau, take your brother back to the car."

But, I should go in with you, Mawmaw," Beau insists.

"Mais, no, someone's got to mind Trent. Go back to the car, Beau. I'll call you in a minute."

Belle enters to find Celestine dead, a needle in her left arm. The document Celestine left on the table—a life insurance policy—sits on the kitchen table. Belle screams. "My baby! Oh, my baby, Celestine. No! No! No! Beau, come quickly."

"I'm coming, Mawmaw."

Beau ushers Trent around to the back of the house and through the back door to avoid passing by their mother, Celestine.

"Trent, you best be going to bed right now. We don't want the Easter Bunny skipping over our house."

Felicia wakes up and comes out of her room. "Will you all be quiet! I'm trying to get some sleep."

Belle wails on the bathroom floor, holding Celestine in her arms.

Beau takes Felicia by the hand, "Felicia. Our Momma's dead."

Felicia screams at the top of her lungs. Beau tries to hold her, but she runs to the front door, throws it open and screams again.

"Mawmaw, I'll call the sheriff," Beau says. "Best before all the neighbors come with Felicia making it everybody's business."

Belle rocks Celestine. "My baby girl. My poor baby girl. The Easter Bunny would never let us down. Look what Trent won! A whole basket of candy." She looks up to the sky and says aloud, "Am I the only one around here who trusts in you, Lord?"

15 Teo Marshall's Wake or Parlor Two

A thunder clap snaps Belle and Goodman from their storytelling. Belle grabs Goodman's arm. He grabs her hand. Goodman looks at her with such sweetness, "Mais, this'll be a night to remember, crois-tu, Ms. Belle?"

"Mais, sûrement."

Johnny Bastien, twenty-eight, Cajun decent, of small stature, but brawny and tanned, pokes his head into the kitchen. "Hello there! You Mr. Morgan? I got the shrimp and the beer for Teo Marshall's wake."

Belle gasps at the sight of him, "My goodness! You're soaked. You look like you were just baptized!"

Johnny Bastien holds a dolly with two kegs of beer. "Well, ma'am, pardon me. I don't go to that church. I was born right the first time. Anyhow, it's looking like the hurricane's comin' up faster than they're sayin'."

Goodman looks out the back. "I best go set up the generator."

Belle asks, "And, son, you are?"

"I'm Johnny, Ma'am." He extends his hand, but realizing how wet and dirty it is, retracts it with a smile. "Sorry about that."

"Johnny, I'm Mrs. Boudreaux. Let me show you where you fellas can set things up."

Belle heads out to the front hallway towards Parlor Two with Johnny and the kegs in tow. In Parlor Two, the shrimpers set up the kegs with red plastic cups, large grease-stained paper bags of hog cracklin's, and two large rice-cookers with steamed boudin sausage.

Leah Marshall, Teo's wife, tiny, buxom, and all of about twenty-five, wears black jeans and a white cotton shirt with a crocheted black vest, enters with Teo's shrimp boots, crawfish trap, his rifle, and a picture of Teo and carrying one of their baby girls on her shoulder, the other one in tow. Leah sets the items down to take Belle's hand. "Ms. Belle, this is so hard. We were going to take the kids to Baton Rouge."

Belle warmly embraces Leah. "You are strong, Mrs. Marshall. Stay strong. The Lord will watch over you and your little angels." Feeling the young widow's pain and wiping tears from Leah's eyes, Belle takes the items. "I'll make this so pretty, Mrs. Marshall. Your husband'll be two-stepping in Heaven."

"My name is Leah Marie, but please call me Leet."

They kiss each other's hands.

"Leet, that's a nice name. You may call me Belle."

"Thank you, chèr Belle." Leet can't stop her tears.

Belle gives her a handkerchief and takes the baby. "Who do we have here?"

Leet smells the handkerchief. "You always smell so good. That's Annabelle. She's the baby." Her other daughter peeks out from behind her leg. "And this one's Michelle."

"Michelle and Annabelle...such pretty names for pretty girls. Sugar, you just go into my purse and spray a little scent on your wrists. Smelling good always makes you feel a little better. I'll take your girls to the kitchen and give Michelle some colors and paper. There's plenty of us in there to hold the baby." Belle leans her head out the door and calls to Beau. "Beau, darling, would you come here? I'm not finished with my florals. Can you keep an eye on Trent and help the shrimpers set their meal up? I'm taking Mrs. Marshall's girls to the kitchen."

"Yes, Mawmaw. Parlor One is all Windexed and polished. I've got all the rosaries set up in there. Everything is fit for the sacrament. Father Gaudet wants the wine on the cellarette by his side of the room. Winston's the alter boy. Here, let me take Teo's things to the back." Beau takes the items that Leet has brought.

"You got them, then, Beau?" Belle asks as she sets them to balance on his arms with her one free arm.

"Yes, I do, Mawmaw." He turns to Leet, "We'll make a nice tribute bouquet for you, Mrs. Marshall. And, I am so sorry for your loss. Your little girls are getting so big!"

"Thank you, Beau," Leet blows her nose in Belle's handkerchief.

Beau checks on Trent, then heads to the back, carrying Leet's items for Belle.

"And, Beau," Belle calls out to him, "bring the umbrella bucket to the front, would you?"

"Yes, Mawmaw."

Goodman comes into Parlor Two, holding a drill. "We'll need to put some towels by the front door, so people can dry off, Miss Belle."

"Beau'll take care of it, Mr. Morgan. You best get those boards up before the wind gets too high. Come on, Michelle. Let's find you some colors." Michelle dutifully takes Belle's free hand and walks back with her to the kitchen.

When Belle gets there, she stands for a moment in the doorway with the girls. "Look who's here."

Ursula dries her hands, "Come over here and give me some sugar, Michelle." She gives the little girl a big hug and rubs her nose to nose. "That's a butterfly kiss, Michelle. You know how to do that? Reginald, look how much she's grown!"

Reginald stoops down to Michelle's eye line. "I am so happy to see you, Michelle. I've got some colors over here by the sideboard. Would you like to draw with me?"

Michelle follows Reginald to the table. Belle passes Annabelle to Ursula, then heads to the back room to finish setting up Teo Marshall's flowers. "Beau, don't forget to put the scent on the towels."

"Rose or jasmine, Mawmaw?"

"Oh! Jasmine, sûrement."

16 Bright Frothy Jello Salads and the Rosary

The wind steps up to a howl and the rain pelts the old funeral home.

Father Gaudet approaches Winston. "We'll be reciting mass soon. Go put on your robes, chèr."

Winston nods, "Yes, Father."

When Winston exits, Father Gaudet takes another sip from his flask.

In the front hallway, the La Reeve guests begin to arrive in droves, refugees from the rain. They come bearing fancy food on high-end Tupperware platters: crawfish bisque, crab cakes, chicken salad sandwiches with the crusts cut off, a ham, fried chicken, and fried catfish. The salads they bear are carrot-raisin-pecan coleslaw; potato salad with green onions, parsley, black pepper and paprika; and fruit salads the color of hibiscus and brides' maid's dresses—pistachio green with cool whip, whipping cream, marshmallows, coconut and pineapples and mint green jello with pecans at the base. One salad is pink jello with maraschino cherries and cherry juice, and another is yellow jello with lemon pudding, oranges and orange slices. All the desserts laid out look like frothy rainbows.

The desserts consist of Seven-up cake, Coca-cola cake, eclairs from Poupart's Bakery on St. Charles Street, and a red velvet cake. And, of course, Ida Marguerite Thomkins comes in with her famous divinity fudge which she swears she only makes up on the occasion of a wake.

When she enters, she cries, "I do declare, my feet are just soaked to the bone!" And then, to Trent, "Why, honey, you are a nice young man. Can you take this from me?"

Trent points her to the Parlor. "The body is in there. Please. Tank you very much."

"Oh, I see. You have a different job. Well, alright, then," Ida Marguerite Thomkins smiles weakly...*I wonder if he can even go to the bathroom on his own.* She stands in a plush pose, holding her jacket, waiting for someone to lift it from her upheld hand, all the while eyeing Parlor One to see where the best place might be for her to be seen close to the body.

"Let me take that from you, Ida Marguerite," Belle lifts her jacket and the divinity fudge from her. Ursula and Odetta take the platters from the guests now pouring in and set them up on the sideboard in Parlor One.

Ida removes her shoes and puts them by the umbrella rack. She's cut the leather out where her bunions are and painted her skin with shoe polish to match where the holes were. "I don't think anyone will mind my bunion paint in this weather, don'tcha think?" she says, looking to Trent for an affirmative response.

Belle glances at the circles of brown on Ida's bunions, "Ida Marguerite, you just make yourself comfortable." *Dear Lord, bless their hearts. Here I am worrying about whether my shoes match and she's wearing shoes with holes. That fudge must be setting her back something....*

Winston looks for Beau. "Trent, where is Beau?"

"Beau be in the k-k-kitchen, please, tank you bery much please."

"Thank you, Trent." Winston, though not without a touch of holier-than-thou-ness in his lexicon, still offsets his mother's caustic presence with a gilded sweetness.

Beau pops out the kitchen door and bumps into Winston. "Hey."

"Hey, Beau. I'm settin' up for the wake."

"You need any help, Winston?"

"Sure."

Beau asks him, "You seen the movie yet?"

"Yeah, I had to sneak to Baton Rouge to see Brokeback."

"You like it?"

"Yeah."

Beau smiles. "Yeah, me, too." Beau points to the bathroom. "Here's where you can change." He opens the bathroom door for Winston.

Winston holds his alter boy cossack.

Beau says, "Don we now our church apparel."

Winston asks, "Do you think it's going to make my ass look big?"

"Accentuate the positive!"

Winston enters the bathroom. He leaves the door part way open. He puts on his robes, combs his hair, looking behind him in the mirror, in case Beau is still there.

Standing to the side, Beau secretly peeks in the open door, watching him.

Winston senses him, turns to look. But, by then, Beau has closed the door.

A pipe organ sits in the corner of Parlor One. The replacement organist, Irma Leboeuf, who has walked over from just past Pop's Gas, plays *Garden of Roses*. When Winston enters, he takes his place next to Father Gaudet. The La Reeve guests, now mostly assembled on wooden fold-out chairs in a circle around the coffin, are poised with their rosaries.

If the walls had ears to hear what the La Reeve guests were all thinking about one another.... As they wait for the Rosary to begin, they silently check one another out. Who's is sitting where and wondering if Mrs. Dubois still has the tag on the rosary she got from the Vatican or if Mr. LaRose would dare use his rosary that had been specially blessed by Father Cournier, whom everyone previously believed walked on the Bayou, before it was found out that the little Catholic girl he'd saved from drowning, he'd also molested on the way out of the water. The Church moved him to a different parish after the incident and it was never discussed again. And over time, these rumors, of course, tend to take on a convoluted form of truth mixed with myth. When the story had played itself out, Father Cournier was more man-devil than priest. But, the rosary was of white luminescent quartz crystal and it was actually quite exquisite. So, Mr. LaRose preferred to accept denial about the history of how it came to be in his possession as he sat there, grinning and holding it in the ready.

As they wait for the Rosary to begin, the guests in Parlor One sip coffee and whisper quiet pleasantries to one another about how wonderful Lawrence La Reeve looks. In fact, he's never looked better (thanks to Belle's make-up job). All the while, they continue to eye one another's rosaries, regarding their status in relation to one another.

Their voices are, however, mostly drowned out by the sounds both of the driving rain on the windows and Goodman's drill as he secures the shutters.

17 Meanwhile...

Popo Cole continues to walk steadily through the driving rain. Soaked, with the tool bag on his back, he balances the shovels over his shoulders, and the sledge hammer in one hand; In the other hand, he holds his rosary.

～　～　～

Belle works her pristine magic on the tribute bouquet up on an easel for Teo Marshall's service. And guests for both parties continue to arrive.

Beau enters the back room where Belle is finishing up the bouquet.

"Those poor shrimpers hardly have a pot to pee in. Beau," Belle says as she fastens the crab cage, surrounded by oleander flowers. Inside the cage are two red plastic shrimp. "I want Mrs. Marshall to have the nicest bouquet here today for her husband. Take those boots, his rifle, and his picture and set them up on his coffin, would you, Honey?"

Beau admires her handiwork. "That is looking nice, Mawmaw." Celestine stands behind Belle.

Celestine speaks to her son, "I saw Winston, Beau. You know, sometimes we're born with certain antennae. That's cause God's angels don't want you to be alone."

"I'm glad my antennae is connected to you, Momma. But, sometimes, I wish you'd just turn down the dial a bit."

"Sometimes, it's tough being that sensitive, Beau. But, you'll get used to it," Celestine laughs.

Belle hears it, but ignores it. Celestine stands by, admiring the tribute bouquet. Then, she says to Belle, "Popo Cole's coming for me, Maman. Today's the day. He promised to bring me home."

Beau and Belle look at Celestine aghast. Belle can't believe her daughter would ask such a thing of her on a day like this. "Celestine Rosalie! No! Why today? You can't do it today! The weather's too hard. I've got too many things to do. My plate's too full already, Sweetie. My plate is just too full to accommodate you today."

But Celestine won't hear it. "Maman, just get a bigger plate, you know, like at the shrimper's buffet." Frustrated by the imposition of her dead daughter's demands, Belle turns back to the bouquet. "Beau, go help Trent greet Teo Marshall's guests."

"Yes, Mawmaw."

As Beau exits, Celestine disappears.

Thunder growls and a clap of lightning causes the lights to blink on and off. As Beau walks down the hallway, the quiet of Parlor One contrasts starkly to the growing ruckus of Teo Marshall's wake in Parlor Two.

Goodman is still outside, putting up boards with his electric drill. Fists of rain beat upon the old house.

As the shrimper guests arrive, each, in their turn, brings something to contribute to the pot luck for their brother shrimper: more boudin, French bread and cane syrup; biscuits; more hog cracklin's and hog's head cheese. The meats on the Parlor Two side of the Azalea Funeral Home this night are fried catfish, a bucket of chicken from Duck's Drive-in, a bucket of oysters, and smoked sausage. There is no green salad. And dessert is jello, vanilla wafers, and banana pudding with no bananas.

Joe Gaspar, one of the older shrimpers, shakes off the rain as he enters, carrying another bag of cracklin's. He thrusts them towards Trent, "My wife made these."

Trent points, "The body's in there, please, tank you bery much."

"Oh, Trent! Hey, chèr, comment ça va? How you be, Trent, huh? You want to share one of my cracklin's."

"Tank you bery much please." Trent takes the cracklin' and devours it.

"Now, Trent, you need to wash your hands, chèr." Lois, Joe's wife, carrying French bread, enters after him, stomping the rain off her shoes. "You afraid of the hurricane, Trent?"

"I not be afraid," he says, licking his fingers.

Aniline, another old shrimper's wife, enters with a pot of Boudin. Aniline's hard-of-hearing. She looks to Joe, inquiring about Trent. "Mais, who's this?"

But, Trent proudly answers for him, "I be Trent Landry."

Behind Joe's back, in a quiet voice, Lois says, "That's Celestine's son."

"Who?"

Louder, Lois yells to her, "Celestine Boudreaux! Remember? Rightly Landry's wife."

"Celestine. Mon Dieu. Mais, non." Aniline embraces Trent. "Chèr, te fils, Trent. Chèr bon Dieu.

Chèr, pauvre bête. Your maman was the prettiest lady in all the parish." Her voice is loud on account of her deafness.

Sister Myers, a member of the La Reeve party, steps out from Parlor One. "Can y'all keep it down out here? This is a sanctimonious event."

As if on cue, a clap of thunder interrupts the sister's voice. Aniline, friendly, almost bowing to her, says, "What did you say, Sister? "

"I said, 'Can y'all keep it down here!'"

Hearing the conflict, Belle comes flying down the hall, carrying Teo's tribute wreath. "I'm sorry, Sister Myers. I'll take care of it." Belle looks for Goodman. "Beau, is Mr. Morgan still outdoors? He is going to catch his death in that rain. Oh, my goodness, Trent. Let's get those hands washed. You been eating already?"

"Mais, Belle, I shared a cracklin' with him," Joe helps her with the wreath.

"That's mighty nice of you, Joe. Thank you. Now, Trent, go wash your hands. I'll mind the front door till you get back."

Goodman steps in just then, soaked to the bone.

Belle grabs a towel, hanging near the umbrella bucket, to wipe off the excess water from Goodman. "Dear Lord! Look at you! You look like you just been in a swimming pool."

Goodman takes it all in stride. "Howdy, folks. I think we're all battened down now. I'll best go change my clothes."

"Goodman, there's a clean shirt and pressed pants in the back room. You could get those." Belle gestures politely indicating he head on back.

Sister Myers returns to Parlor One. Before she enters the parlor, she leans out to Beau, "Just make sure they don't eat our food."

"Would you care for another cup of coffee, Sister?" Beau holds up the pot of coffee in an offering.

"You'll need to bring in more than a cup for me. We're outta' woman's coffee in our Parlor," the nun snaps.

Upon hearing this, Belle thinks, *Not the nuns, too! Again, I thank you, Lord. You have guided me and spared me from those dreadful La Reeves!*

Trent returns and Belle reflexively inspects his hands. In her most gracious voice, as if to model proper courtesy, "Beau, would you kindly make more for Mr. La Reeve's party. We certainly don't want the Lord's servants running out of coffee."

"No, we don't. Do we Mawmaw?" he quips, not half kidding. "I am an Azalea maid at their service." He curtsies. Belle makes a sign of the cross. Beau exits towards the kitchen.

She calls back to him, "And, don't forget to get the men's blend."

18 Back in the Kitchen or My Feet Hurt

Leet's five-year-old daughter, Michelle, sits on Reginald's lap. She draws with crayons and he reads his history textbook.

She stops what she's doing and points to a picture of a Choctaw woman in his book, walking along the Trail of Tears. "Who's that? She's pretty."

Reginald tears a piece of paper and draws a girl's face on it and tapes it onto her finger—a finger puppet. And then, he does the same to his, but draws a boy, and tells her a story about them.

"Hold your finger up, Michelle. You be the lady in the picture. She's a Choctaw mommy." He holds his puppet finger up. "And I'll be the Choctaw daddy. A long long time ago, this mommy and daddy lived not too far from here. You want to see where they lived?"

"Yes," she nods.

He turns to a map in the back of his book. "We're here, right now. Here's where they lived, at the top of Louisiana. That's called the North."

Michelle points to the water. "My daddy lives here." She points on the map to the Gulf waters.

Reginald's heart skips a beat. Ursula gives him a look that says *You better take this one nice and easy, Baby.* Reginald says, "You're right. He works on a boat, doesn't he?"

She smiles. "Mmmmhmmm. A big boat with fish!"

And that's all the information he needs to know that little Michelle does not know her daddy's not coming home.

"There are fish on that boat? That's something! The lady in the picture couldn't stay where she was living because the government said she had to move away."

"Where'd she go?"

"She had to start walking and she walked and walked and walked." Reginald puts his finger puppet next to hers and mimes walking with it.

"Did her feet hurt?" Michelle asks.

"Oh, yes. Their feet hurt a lot." He pantomimes his puppet's feet hurting, "Ouch! Ouch! Ouch!" And she echoes him, "Ouch! Ouch! Ouch!"

Ursula, holding Annabelle, talks to Reginald by talking to the baby, "Annabelle, I like to tell happy stories. Don't you?"

"Oh, Mama, don't worry. It's a love story. So, as I was saying, Michelle, they walked so far that their feet hurt a lot."

Michelle jumps her puppet up and down again, "Ouch! Ouch! Ouch!"

Leet comes in to get the baby. "Miss Ursula, thank you for holding Annabelle. I can take her for now."

"My pleasure. What an easy baby." Ursula passes Annabelle back to her mother.

'Oh, yes, she is easy. Both my girls are easy." Leet looks at Michelle and Reginald. "What you doing, Shelley?"

Michelle holds up her finger and repeats, "Ouch! Ouch! Ouch! My feet hurt, just like Daddy."

Reginald explains, "I'm the Choctaw daddy and I just walked a long way. And she's the Choctaw mommy and she walked a long way, too. Our feet are hurtin' bad." Then, he turns back to Michelle and says, "But, you know what hurt more than their feet?"

"Nuhuh." She shakes her head.

His puppet says, "My heart is so sad! It hurts more than my feet."

"More?" Michelle asks.

"Yes." He makes his puppet stand next to hers. "Do you know where your heart is?" He points to her heart. "It's right there. Can you feel it?"

She thinks for a moment. "Yes."

"Let's sit down here a while and rest our feet a spell," his puppet says.

"Okay," she giggles, holding her puppet next to his.

"Oh, that feels so good," he smiles, "No more pain."

"Mine, neither."

"But my heart is still sad," he says.

"Me, too."

"Oh, yeah? Why is your heart sad?" Reginald's puppet asks her puppet.

Her finger puppet says, "My daddy's on a boat and I am always sad until he comes back."

"My daddy's not here, either," his puppet says. "But he is always in my heart, no matter where I am. If you listen, you can always feel your daddy in your heart." He points. "Right there."

She cocks her head as if she's listening. "I can feel him."

"That's good, Shelley. Maybe we can keep each other company while we wait. Would you like that?"

"Yes." She leans deeper into Reginald's chest. He looks to Leet. "She's a nice little girl. And did you see her drawing?"

The drawing is of a mommy and daddy and two girls and a boat, some clouds and rainbows and a smiling sun with sun rays beaming down on the family.

Leet looks at it, choking back tears. "When should I say?"

Together, Ursula and Reginald emphatically indicate: NOT YET.

Ursula adds, "You go on back in. This precious angel can stay in the kitchen with us."

19 The Mourners

In Parlor Two, with the wreath set up, Belle checks on Teo's coffin. Everything is in place. His boots on the lid below the waist, rifle positioned on the open lid. Everything is just so.

Every shrimper who shows up also brings in fresh shrimp to be boiled. Belle runs around, lighting Sternos and sets up the food on the hot plates. The shrimper's guests cry and hug with beers in their hands...

And then one of them begins to sing *J'ai passé devant ta porte*... and they all join in A Capella.

> *J'ai passé devant ta porte*
> *J'ai crié "bye-bye" à mon beau*
> *Y'a personne qui m'a répondu*
> *Oh yé yaille, mon coeur fait mal*
> *Quand je m'ai mis à observer*
> *Là j'ai vu des chandelles allumées*
> *Tout le tour de son cercueil*
> *Oh yé yaille, mon coeur est malade*

In Parlor One, the solemnity is thick with ceremony. Here, Mrs. Tale Dule-Richarde, on the Liturgical committee and who is head teacher of the girl's confirmation class at St. Luke's Catholic Church, is about to recite *The Glory Be*.

As the resident expert in all things Virgin Mother Mary, Mrs. Dule-Richarde is naturally given the honor of the recitation. She is, after all, the one who has chosen the Mary to be studied for New Iberia white girls for every confirmation class for the last twenty-seven years...Our Lady of Fatima, Our Lady of Lourdes, Our Lady of Grace and so on.... And everyone knows she's the most bookish woman in the congregation at the church and is unchallenged in her capacity for research. The La Reeve guests can't help but to hold her as someone whose status they both envy for her precision and equally abhor for the dryness of her recitation.

Standing at the back and along the sides of Parlor One are also the Knights of Columbus, as Lawrence La Reeve was a brother Knight of the Order. They drink a private blend of coffee during the recitation—Belle's "Special Blend" (for the men only), which consists of a fifth of Crown Royal bourbon, one half cup of Wild Turkey bourbon, and a splash of Stein's cane molasses. When you stir it all together, it looks just like coffee.

Belle keeps it hidden in the refrigerator, premixed and ready to go.

Beau holds the men's coffee pot. And the men await with their cups poised for a proper pour, while Father Gaudet follows Beau down the line. Beau makes sure that the Father's cup is always full. And Father Gaudet fans the top and whispers to him, "C'est chaux. Tell your Mawmaw she makes such good coffee."

Before formally introducing Mrs. Dule-Richarde, Father Gaudet sets his cup momentarily on the sideboard and begins, "We are gathered together to pray for Lawrence La Reeve, to keep his memory under the watchful eye of Christ, to remember the mysteries in the history of our salvation, and to thank and praise God for them. There are twenty mysteries reflected upon in the Rosary. Mr. La Reeve expressed a wish to be remembered with the Glorious Mysteries."

Father Gaudet makes the sign of the cross. Everyone follows. "Let us begin. Our Father, who art in Heaven...."

After the *Our Father*, he steps back from the limelight and aligns himself with the Knights. Mrs. Dule-Richarde takes over. She dons her glasses. "We shall now be doing the sacred mysteries..." If her voice weren't so flat, her presence would be distracting in its erudition. "Glory be to the Father, and to the Son, and to the Holy Spirit. As it was in the beginning, is now, and ever shall be. World without end. Amen."

The Knights echo "Amen" and sip their coffees.

"The first glorious mystery was the Resurrection. The body of Jesus is placed in the tomb on the evening of Good Friday...."

The Knights echo, "Amen." Sip....

And while Mrs. Dule-Richarde drones on, the Knights continue to fan their iced bourbon and the La Reeve guests, heads bowed, steep themselves in the Rosary.

The Gulf gale howls.

And Father Gaudet is wafting three sheets to the wind.

~ ~ ~

Popo Cole arrives.

He stands behind the Azalea Funeral Home in the driving rain, searches for the tomb of Celestine near the sun porch.

Hearing *J'ai passé devant ta porte*, he sings along.

He hears the Rosary and recites that, too, along with the other group of mourners.

He searches the sky for a sign.

Thunder claps.

Celestine is illuminated by a flash of lightning.

She points to her grave.

20 Home or Evangeline

Felicia goes to make herself a plate of food on the La Reeve side of the funeral parlor. She only dishes out large shrimp, crab, and gumbo. Beau stands by the door.

Celestine whispers into Beau's ear and Beau says to her, "Hey, Felicia, they have your favorite in Parlor Two. Cracklin's and Hog Head Cheese."

Felicia goes to Beau quietly. "You're gonna pay for that. I'd watch my back when you get off the bus tomorrow."

"There isn't going to be any school tomorrow, Felicia. Hurricane's going to blow through."

Beau steps into Parlor Two and grabs himself a hand full of cracklin's. He holds them up threateningly over Felicia's bisque. Frozen, however, by his need to look and be perfect, he just can't bring himself to drop them into her bisque. Felicia pre-empts him by dumping her bisque on top of his head. In an effort to hide his hurt feelings, he licks his face. "Mmmm... Mmmm... Delicious. I'm going to get some French bread and enjoy my gumbo."

Felicia storms back to the kitchen.

Beau grabs a towel from the front and heads out to the sun porch to clean off his shirt and lick his wounds. Seeing the food on Beau's shirt, Reginald steps out from the kitchen as Beau runs by. "Oh, Beau! What happened to you?" He puts his hands on Beau's shoulders. Beau fights back tears. "It's okay to cry, my brother. Come here." Reginald tries to wrap his big arm around his friend, but Beau pulls back.

"Reginald, I refuse to soil your shirt." Beau releases from Reginald's grasp and runs to the sun porch, weeping.

On the porch, two stray dogs appear and lick the food off his shirt. Still crying, Beau pets the dogs. All this time, Reginald is looking at him from the screen door.

Celestine appears to Beau. "I need you to be strong. You are the man of the house. And you have to take me home."

Beau snaps back, "We don't have a home. We never had a home, Momma."

But, Celestine presses on. "My precious angel, let me tell you about home. Let me show you what home is."

Thunder booms.

Celestine takes Beau's hand and leads him out into the graveyard. Ghostly images light up the rain. He doesn't see Popo Cole who is standing to the side, reciting the Rosary.

Celestine lets go of Beau's hand. She moves quickly from grave to grave. Beau watches with rapt attention. "Now, looky here, Beau." Fire flashes on the tops of a group of graves. "British soldiers burned the homes of the Acadian and Mi'kmaq people. Our people. Our homes."

Celestine points to another grave. There stands Gabriel. "Gabriel and his Acadian wife, Evangeline, are driven apart." A British soldier appears and drives a bayonet between the apparitions, separating Gabriel and Evangeline.

"After they were separated in Acadia, Evangeline ended up in Philadelphia, always looking for Gabriel." Celestine, as Evangeline, searches desperately and despairingly between the gravestones. "She eventually gave up and became a nun, working at a hospital there."

Evangeline, as nun, goes to another grave. By now, the whole graveyard off the sunporch is a theatre of spirits. A corpse rises to play an infirmed patient.

"Then, one day, at the hospital, Evangeline encountered Gabriel. By this time, he was an old man." Gabriel rises up from one of the graves. Evangeline and Gabriel embrace. "He tells her, 'Our people are hiding in the Bayou Teche.' And, Gabriel dies in Evangeline's arms." Celestine disappears.

Lightning flashes on the tree by Celestine's grave.

Celestine's voice can be heard through the rain, "The Indians were driven out of their homes, too."

Cherokee people walk slowly through the graveyard, chanting sadly.

The two dogs bark furiously.

Thunder crashes. Lightning flashes. Celestine sits on another grave, watching. "Evangeline went insane and died. But, Beau, years later, when they dug up her grave, just like Jesus, she wasn't there. The Lord, in His mercy, had called her home."

Through his tears, Beau sees Popo Cole reciting the Rosary by Momma Celestine's grave.

Celestine stands by with her hand on Beau's shoulder, watching her father—Popo Cole—pray in the driving rain.

She says to Beau, "Remember what I asked you long ago, Beau? Do you remember? You gotta help me. I'm going home tonight, Son, just like Evangeline.

Reginald, who has been watching the whole time and seeing the apparitions, comes out and puts his hand on Beau's other shoulder. With his other hand outstretched to the sky, he sings "Wayfaring Stranger" in the rain. But this time, he's not goofing around.

> *I'm just a poor wayfarin' stranger,*
> *While travelin' through this world below.*
> *Yet there's no sickness, no toil, nor danger,*
> *In that bright land to which I go.*
> *I'm goin' there to see my Father.*
> *And all my loved ones who've gone on.*
> *I'm just goin' over Jordan.*
> *I'm just goin' over home.*

21 Outta' Shrimp

Through the window, Ursula sees Reginald's arms stretched up in the rain. "Good Lord in Heaven, what is he doing out in that storm? Out singing in the rain? Reginald Robeson Washington, get you inside!"

Reginald sees her looking at him, points to the graveyard. But, Ursula doesn't see what he's seeing. She wipes her hands on her apron and heads out to bring him in.

The shrimpers continue to bring in fresh shrimp.

Every boiling pot is being used on the stove and over Sterno on the counter.

Belle pulls Goodman aside. "Goodman, at the rate they're cooking shrimp in the kitchen and in Parlor Two, the whole funeral home's going to smell like the Gulf."

"Well, I can't open the windows in this weather, Belle."

"You got a propane tank we can set up somewhere?"

Goodman thinks for a moment. "I can back the hearse out of the carport and they can cook all the shrimp they can eat in there. My daddy always brought shrimp into the carport in a storm. That way, we just watched the city blow by."

"Alrighty, I'll move 'em over to cook out there, then," she says.

Beau enters the kitchen, followed by Reginald.

Belle gasps at the sight of them, "What happened to your shirts, gentlemen?"

"Thought I'd try Japanese print painting. But, it just didn't work out."

"The Battle of Felicia?"

"Nevermind, Mawmaw. Just collateral damage."

Goodman chimes in, "I got some clean shirts you boys can wear, Beau, Reginald. Miss Belle always presses me a couple of extra shirts when it gets too hot. You gentlemen go up there and change into those dry clothes."

"They're in the closet next to Mr. Morgan's office," Belle calls after them. Beau and Reginald, like wet dish rags, dutifully head up the stairs to Mr. Morgan's office.

Belle looks at Ursula, "How can anyone live with an angel and a devil and not go mad? Just like my daughter, I understand so much more now than I used to."

Johnny Bastien enters, "Mrs. Boudreaux, we're outta' shrimp in the parlor. A couple of us boys are going to Gloria's locker to pick up some more."

"In this weather? Johnny! Now, look here, Mr. Morgan's fixing to set up a tank in the carport. When you come back, y'all can set your cooking up there. I'm moving the Sternos out there when you go. Alrighty?"

"Alrighty, Ma'am."

Goodman hops to. "I'll go move the hearse out of there, now."

Johnny flashes his warm smile, "This'll be great! I love cookin' in the rain!"

Goodman, standing at the doorway, suggests it might not be the best idea for him to fetch any more shrimp. "Johnny, it's blowin' too hard to drive your truck."

"I thought of that one already, Mr. Morgan. I brought the semi-. It's parked out front. I know it's big for a couple of lockers of shrimp. But, at least, we won't blow over and everyone can keep eating tonight. No one's going home in this weather and the shrimp boats won't be going out tomorrow morning, neither." He tips his hat, but waits to hear the radio before he heads out into the wet night.

Goodman checks the radio: "Morgan City's in the eye of the hurricane. One hundred and forty five mile an hour winds. Landfall in New Iberia expected shortly."

A sudden quiet comes over the staff in the kitchen. Ursula breaks the silence. "That hurricane's headed for New Iberia? It'll be Katrina all over again!"

Goodman turns the radio down. "Johnny, are you sure you wanna' get that shrimp?"

"Yessir. It's only a swing around a couple of blocks here and everyone'll be fed until the storm subsides, even your guests on the other side."

"That's mighty kind of you to think of them," Belle tells Johnny. "I'd best get more coffee on."

The lights blink on and off.

22 The Help and The Guests or The Storm Heightens

Ursula leaves the kitchen for the Ladies Room. "Mama Odetta, can you take my place in the dining area and kitchen? I need to dry off."

Just then, Shareen walks in. "What are you doing, messing up my bathroom?" She sniffs the air. "Is somebody washing a dog?"

Ursula steps in front of her mother, "Mama, go on out there and help me out as I asked." To Shareen, "The floor 'll be clean in two minutes, Ms. La Reeve."

Shareen glares at Ursula's wet shoulders and sniffs again. "No, I was talkin' about the dog. There's a dog in here. I can smell it."

Shareen is just looking for something to be wrong. "Why is the floor all wet? Don't you niggers have towels? And don't you be throwing newspaper on this tile floor."

Belle rushes to accommodate Shareen. "I'm sorry. Be careful. No slipping. I'll take care of it. Mrs. Washington is here to cook, not clean, Shareen." Belle gets on her hands and knees to dry the floor where

Ursula's wet clothes have dripped. Shareen stands over her for a minute, enjoying her moment of power.

Odetta returns to the kitchen with Shareen breathing down her neck. Beau and Reginald show up in Goodman's pressed white shirts that don't fit them and neckties that go half way down their thighs.

Reginald asks, "Where's Mama?"

Odetta, "She's cleaning up in the bathroom, Reginald."

Shareen barks, "Well, she best clean the commodes while she's in there and better than she does at my house. And d'y'all have anything to take that smell outta' heah?" She goes under the cabinet and takes a can of Lysol.

Reginald deliberately reaches across in front of her and takes out Pier One Import "Apple Pear" sachet spray. With his big gap-toothed grin, he holds it up for her. "Oh, ma'am, we use this in our house. It's *very* fragrant."

"In my house, your momma scrubs my floor."

They all just stare at her, speechless in the wake of her gall.

A La Reeve guest comes into the kitchen to talk to Belle, "Can y'all get them to turn that chanky-chank down? We're trying to honor the dead."

Johnny hears that as he walks in with the shrimp he's fetched for everyone. "We're trying to honor the dead here, too. Would you care for some shrimp, Ma'am?"

Guests keep arriving. Everyone's talking about the storm. The radio is up high in Parlor Two and the weather report can be heard in the Front Hallway.

Radio: *Rita has made landfall in Southwestern Louisiana with wind speeds up to one hundred and forty-five miles per hour.*

And the chanky-chank music cranks on, filling up the funeral home with frenzied merriment, Cajun style.

Beau heads to the front to help Trent. As more and more guests arrive, he greets them with grace and ease, "May I take your jackets?"

Belle enters, carrying a coffee pot and a tray of cups.

One guest says to Trent, "Don't be afraid, Trent."

"I not be afraid."

A thunderclap. Everyone jumps. Trent doesn't flinch.

"I said I not be afraid."

Goodman assures them, "This house has been here since 1863. It made it through Camille and Katrina. It will make it through this. I best go check the generator." Belle touches his arm. "Goodman, put an overall on and leave your good suit coat in here this time, ça-va, chèr?"

The house creaks. Shutters slam. Felicia enters, freaked out. The lights go on and off. "Mawmaw, you have to take me home."

"Sweetie, when the weather's like this, the sheriff isn't going to let anyone out on the road unless it's very very important."

"Well, I'm important."

Celestine stands by Belle, "C'est le guerre, Maman."

Felicia picks up the house phone in an attempt to call a friend, but the line is dead.

Murmuring can be heard from both parlors. "I hope it's not going to be another Katrina." "Mon Dieu! Qu'est-ce que la pluie!"

Some of the La Reeve guests take a break from the Rosary to drink coffee in the hallway and chat, "Katrina ruined the sugar cane fields. Now, Rita's going to kill us." "Jesus will get us through it." "If they put the TV cameras on the Black folks, no one's gonna' send any money."

Branches and flying things start hitting the sides of the Funeral Home. A shutter can be heard coming off its hinges.

Goodman, fresh in from starting the generator, pivots to head back out. "And now, I best fix that shutter before it blows away."

23 Here's To Teo Marshall

Johnny Bastien raises his glass. "I think we're all gathered here now, Teo's family and friends. I just want to say that Teo Morgan was the best young fisherman in our fleet. He could walk on the Bayou, the Basin, the Gulf...any water, 'cept the day he didn't, which is the occasion of this gathering."

Shrimper Bruté calls out, "Here's to Teo's laugh. I can hear him now. He's laughing at us from his lawn chair me made, so he could drink his beer and not get wet in the rain."

"And keep his boudin fresh," another voice affirms his sentiment.

The Shrimper Guests raise their glasses and drink to that. "Here! Here!"

Bruté continues, "I'm going to miss drivin' by your trailer and seeing Teo in the kitchen window at night, holding Annabelle on one shoulder, with Michelle sitting on the counter and him showing her how to make gumbo."

Leet wipes back tears. "Thank you all for all the support and love you've given me and our family these last few days. I just want to say that. And, also, that Teo knew that he was loved. He was loved by his blood family. But, also by the family here. All y'all who helped loadin' the traps, all y'all who helped him when his motor broke on the Pero."

Shrimper Leon weighs in, "When my daddy died, Teo taught me how to shave and how to catch crawfish and crabs."

And Shrimper Kent, "Teo rescued us from our roof after Katrina."

And Shrimper Don, "Teo brought us some water after Katrina. I am sure that up in Heaven, Teo's cooking a good sauce piquant right this minute."

Bruté, "Well, he mighta' thought it was undue, Leet. But, he deserved all the attention he got."

Johnny looks over at his friend in the coffin, "Teo, you have a little talk with God and ask him to have those FEMA shitasses come and help us poor Cajuns. Everybody's sending help to N'Oleans. But, they forget about us. But Teo, you never forgot about nobody."

Everyone calls out, "Here! Here!"

Johnny pipes in, "Alrighty, who's ready for gumbo?"

24 Celestine's Grave

The storm rages on.

Outside, ankle deep in water, Popo Cole's sledge hammer hits the side of Celestine's sepulcher, cracking the marble side.

Celestine stands on top, playfully holding the pose of an angel. She sings to Popo Cole:

I'm goin' there to see my Father.
And all my loved ones who've gone on.
I'm just goin' over Jordan.
I'm just goin' over home.

25 This Little Light of Mine

The generator goes out. Everything goes black.

In the hallway, Beau feels his way to the large closet, "Uh, oh...time for some alternative lighting." Beau fetches a box of flashlights from the closet and distributes them. As he passes them out, he sings, "This little light of mine, I'm going to let it shine..."

Trent chimes in. "Shine. Shine. Shine."

Shareen leans out of Parlor One. "We gotta finish our Rosary, Beau. Give us all them flashlights."

Beau feigns horror, "What, Shareen? You don't have the Rosary memorized?"

Belle comes in, holding a candle. "Beau, you know where the hurricane lamps are. Go fetch them. I'll finish distributing these flashlights. Get the candles, too."

One of the La Reeve guests calls out in the dark, "Let that coon-ass trash use the candles. We're in the middle of praying to the Lord."

Bruté calls back from Parlor Two, "Shrimp and crab in your gumbo be coming from my pond, Sister."

Beau amps up the singing and the shrimpers join in. *"This little light of mine. I'm gonna let it shine..."*

Belle joins in, trying to cheer everyone up.

Shrimper Joe goes over to Trent, "Trent, give us a flashlight over here. Venez ici. Ici."

Shareen shrieks, "One of you, get out there and put on that generator. I didn't pay to do my Rosary in the dark."

Goodman, who's found his tools, heads out the door. To Belle, "Give me like five, ten, minutes. There are some more candles under the stairwell."

Belle lights the candles she's got and places them along the shrimper side.

Shareen comes out from the Rosary and snaps at Belle, "I'm glad to see you-know-who's used to living in the dark."

The La Reeve guests laugh.

Belle's had it with Shareen. "'How long will you judge unjustly and show partiality to the wicked?'" As she speaks the words of the Bible, she slowly illuminates the room, handing candles to and lighting all the shrimpers' candles.

To Leet, Belle lovingly recites, "'Defend the weak and the fatherless.'" To Bruté, "'...uphold the cause of the poor and the oppressed. Rescue the weak and needy; Deliver them out of the hand of the wicked. They do not know nor do they understand; They walk about in darkness; All the foundations of the Earth are shaken.'"

When she is finished, the shrimpers raise their candles towards Shareen.

Belle continues, "'I said, You are gods. And all of you are sons of the Most High.'"

The shrimpers, in unison, say Amen.

Winston comes out in his robe, looks for Beau. "That was awesome, Psalm Eighty-two."

Beau quips, "Verse Five."

Winston apologies on behalf of his mother, "Beau, I'm sorry."

Beau gives him a sly smile, "Oh, Père! Pardonne-leur!"

"I love Longfellow!" Winston relishes in another moment of gleeful connection with Beau in what has otherwise been an ominously solemn and very trying night for him. Then, he ducks back into Parlor One, followed by one of the shrimper's wives who has also gone into Parlor One to help herself to a battery flashlight.

26 The Storm Rages On

The shrimpers have taken over the kitchen, pots on every surface, washing plates, piling them up high.

Shrimper Joe: "Fils de puté."

His wife elbows him: "Souhaitez-vous les écouter!"

The radio announces: *Hurricane tracker: Rita's made landfall.*

Belle places a battery lamp in the bathroom. Celestine appears in the mirror. "The storm will be passing over soon. I'm coming home, Mama. The storm will be passing over..."

Belle touches the mirror and Celestine touches back. "Trent won an Easter basket that night, you know, Celestine."

"I thought my insurance policy would take care of y'all. I'm sorry, Mama. I didn't know it didn't work that way."

"I figured that. I forgive you, Celestine. But, I sure do miss you." Celestine fades from the mirror. Belle takes a moment to catch her breath. She primps her hair, sucks in her tummy, straightens her blouse, and heads back to the kitchen, humming, *"The Storm is Passing Over."*

Belle puts on a rain coat, "Thank the Lord, everyone's got light. But, I'm worried about Goodman. I'm going to see if I can help him, Ursula."

Ursula, re-filling the coffee pots, "You're not going out in that rain!"

In the background, the radio is static now with garbled words. *"Czhzzztssssz... Rita....jtzchs... landfall... czhzzztssssz...."*

"I've got to check on Goodman." Belle heads out the back. She makes her way around the side of the house to the generator where Goodman is cranking the shaft, and yells to Goodman. "Goodman! Goodman! You need some help?"

Goodman's holding forth. "Belle, you best get back inside. I'll be alright." He keeps pulling on the start crank to get the generator engine going. Just as it starts up, Belle's wig is sucked off her head by the high winds. Belle reaches out for it and looses her balance. Goodman grabs her arm to keep her from falling.

"Oh, my stars, Goodman. I've got to get my wig!"

"Belle, chèr, that wig is done sucked into the vortex. Hang on, we're going back in." Belle searches through the rain to see if her wig has, perhaps, fallen to the ground. But, Goodman is right. It's gone with the wind.

Whatever solid thing they can steady themselves on, Belle and Goodman make their way back along the side of the house. Holding onto one another, Belle buries her head against Goodman's large chest. Even in the rain, she can smell the air conditioning on his shirt and a faint scent of Bay Rum cologne.

28 The Sepulcher

In the graveyard in the back, off the sun porch, Beau and Reginald, directed by Popo Cole, dig around Celestine's grave with shovels.

Popo Cole directs his grandson, "We got to get the door open, Beau."

The marble on the side finally gives way.

Popo Cole instructs his grandson, "Beau, crawl in there and get your Momma Celestine. I'll pull her from here."

Beau crawls in. Celestine is wrapped in a moldy shroud. He lies next to his mother's body. The sound and chaos of his life outside the sepulcher is momentarily suspended in the silence of this, his mother's tomb.

He spends a moment of communion with her cold body. Then, he takes a deep breath and pushes on Celestine's shoulders.

"Pull, Popo! Pull!"

Popo pulls Celestine out. Holding her in his strong grasp, Popo Cole tears open the shroud with a knife, exposing her skull.

Celestine has made a little daisy chain crown. She places it on the head of her decomposing body. Pointing to it, she says, "Beau, look. Lagniappe!" Then, to her father, she says, "Thank you, Popo." The apparition of Celestine kisses her dead self and she walks off into the stormy night.

Goodman, soaked to the bone, and Belle, sans wig, enter through the front door like apparitions themselves, in from the tempest.

Beau, Reginald, and Popo Cole enter from the back. Popo carries Celestine's body through the hallway. The lights come back on.

The storm stops. They are in the eye. Everything is suddenly quiet.

The Rosary and the festivities of the shrimpers stop. Everybody looks at the spectacle of the Landry-Boudreaux family.

Belle is astonished to see Popo Cole. He smiles sweetly at her, "Long time, chèr. How you be?"

"Cole, Gentlemen, what are y'all doing?"

Trent looks on, "Mudder go home." Wiping the rain and dirt from his face, Beau looks at Belle. "Can't you see?"

"Yes," Belle understands.

Popo Cole says, "We gotta take our baby girl home."

Belle kneels down by Celestine's body, unable to maintain her composure any longer. She weeps as any mother would weep for her dead child. Popo holds Celestine with her. Together, they rock the dirty wet shrouded body of their daughter. Beau kneels next to Belle and, because her wig is gone, kisses her head. "You have a beautiful head, Mawmaw."

"Oh, Beau..."

Trent touches Goodman's arm, "C-c-c-could you take Mudder home, p-p-please?"

Belle introduces Popo Cole and Goodman. "Monsieur Goodman Morgan, Monsieur Cole Maurice Boudreaux."

Goodman, welcoming as ever, "Comment ça-va, chèr?"

"Comme-ci comme-ça, chèr," Popo Cole replies.

Goodman takes over. "Let's get Celestine into the hearse."

Shareen snaps, "You are not going to put that disgusting sinner in the back of your hearse. Not the hearse my daddy's goin' to be ridin' in."

The shrimpers have had enough of her.

Johnny, who's just come in with cases of shrimp, tells everyone, "They're not allowing anyone on the road. The hearse ain't gonna' make it anyways. It's three foot of water to anywhere. It's going to get worse."

A pregnant silence pervades. Then, he says, "Let's put her in my eighteen wheeler outside."

Beau jumps up. "I'll get some towels."

Shareen curses Belle, "A plague has been set upon this house. Cast this darkness out of this house!"

Goodman steps between Shareen and Belle. "I will ask you not to address Mrs. Boudreaux in such a manner. She is our maid of mercy. Together, we are the Azalea Funeral Home. And we honor *all* the dead."

But Shareen's teeth are bared, "Not a mother that kills herself and abandons her children."

Belle's hackles rise up. "My daughter has more spirit and love in her than you will ever feel or have in your alive life, Shareen La Reeve. Judge not lest ye be judged."

"Don't you dare quote the scripture while your hands are so wet with the Devil."

The cat fight is on. "I already did. Remember? Psalm Eighty-two." She blows off Shareen and turns to Goodman. "Shall we?"

One by one, the shrimpers reach up to carry Celestine like pall bearers. Reginald joins in.

Bruté, to the shrimper crowd in Parlor Two, "We're gonna make sure that she gets the right burial. Venez ici, chèrs."

Belle gets in the last word to Shareen, "You are burying your father and everything is taken care of. It is now time for me to bury my daughter."

Goodman seconds the motion. "Amen." To Shareen, he says, "Ms. La Reeve, I've done my best to help your family. Now, I'm doing my best to help my family." To Winston, "Winston, you are in charge here until I get back."

Winston protests, "But, what if something goes wrong?" ...as if nothing's gone wrong already.

Beau assures him, "I think you're readily adaptable to any situation, Winston."

Smiling, Winston agrees, "Indeed. "

The shrimpers sing.

> *Amazing Grace... how sweet the sound*
> *that fills a wretch like me.*
> *I once was lost, but now I'm found.*
> *T'was blind, but now I see.*

By now, all the La Reeve guests are completely aghast, due to the gruesome visage of the exhumed body of Celestine.

Felicia, who has been hiding in the kitchen, enters the hallway and throws a fit. Pointing at Winston, she howls, "I'm not staying here with him."

"Felicia Marie, you stay right here till I get back," Belle commands.

Shareen stomps, "This place is cursed." She points her false-nailed finger at Popo Cole, "That there's a conjuring man."

Ignoring Shareen and the La Reeve party, the shrimpers take over. As they carry Celestine out the front door to the semi-truck, Shareen screams, "This is a house of sin. This is a house of darkness. You can't sing hymns to those who haven't been saved. She's not saved. She's not saaaaaved!"

Father Gaudet sticks his head out, intending to quell the commotion. Trent reaches for his hand. "Father Son Holy Spirit. Save Momma." The Father hesitates for a moment, bows his head, checks in with the Lord, takes a swig from his flask and turns to Shareen, "Ms. La Reeve, I believe the Lord has called me to help these dear souls. Winston can finish the Rosary."

Winston balks, "But, Father..."

Father Gaudet blesses Winston with the sign of the cross. "Animus dominus, you're ordained. Amen." He takes his sash and places it over Winston's shoulders.

So moved by Trent's plea, Father Gaudet grabs an umbrella and follows the body out, holding Trent's hand.

29 To the Burial

Outside the Azalea Funeral Home, the shrimpers and Reginald lay Celestine in the back of the semi-truck. Belle, Beau, Trent, Goodman, Reginald, Father Gaudet and a few shrimpers surround Celestine, all settled in the back on the bags of rice. A knowing look exchanges between Belle and Popo Cole.

"Thank you, Cole."

"Thank you, chèr Belle. When our work is done here, I won't be troubling you again." He gives her a long sweet look and then shuts the door and heads to the cab.

Johnny Bastien sets himself up at the steering wheel of the cab of the semi-, turns on the ignition. "This baby's never let me down."

Popo Cole enters into the front with him. But the truck doesn't start. Cole slaps the dashboard. "Mon Dieu!" It starts.

The storm starts up again.

Back at the Funeral Home, Shareen offers Felicia a ride, "I'll take you home, honey. They are trash. A precious girl like you has no business being raised with a retard and a queer." Shareen and Felicia escape into the night in Shareen's car.

The radio on Shareen's car plays Willie Nelson's "On the Road Again."

But, they've lost the moment. The eye of the hurricane is finished and the other side of the storm takes off. "I know a short cut. I'll get you home faster than you can imagine." Shareen guns it. They pass the Miracle of Mother Mary Bridge sign...

Thunder....

Belle, Beau, Trent, Goodman, Reginald, shrimpers and Father Gaudet, sitting on the rice bags, knock around as the truck heads out into the storm. Goodman comforts Belle who is completely beside herself at this point. "I always knew Celestine was my special child. She could talk to the animals. She could walk outside and, oh, the birds would sing all around her. She had that gift. And, she could look right into your eyes and see right into your soul. That was Celestine."

All the while, Father Gaudet has been silently reciting the rosary. He looks up and says, "Sometimes God puts angels among us who are just too sensitive to walk on the Earth plane. A lot of 'em drown out their feelings with the drink. Pauvres âmes." He raises his flask to them and takes a slug himself.

"Father, I did everything I could to protect my baby," Belle confesses. "But, when Trent was born, and after his seizures and his spinal meningitis, my daughter just couldn't handle it."

Beau hugs his grandmother, "She was a good mother, Mawmaw. She still is. I talk to her all the time."

Trent rocks, "Mawmaw, no cry."

Goodman lets Belle lean on him, "I didn't know her, but I see her in all of your eyes. And it's an honor to bear witness to the most remarkable love of your family, chèr."

Belle sighs, "Suffering does make us stronger. But, why are we seared with so many scars?"

"Mawmaw," Beau says, "We rise up from the battlefield. We are resilient. We are Cajun."

Goodman, patting Belle's wet head, "And the Good Lord always looks at the heart, Ms. Belle. Father, would you please do the honors?"

As they drive into the night towards the cane field, Father Gaudet's voice can be heard, administering a baptism over Celestine. "I bless this angel, Celestine Rosalie Jolie Marie Boudreaux Landry...."

With his usual dramatic flair, Beau adds, "Good night, sweet princess. And flights of angels sing thee to thy rest."

30 Stillness

The ghost of Celestine waits at the cane field. When they drive up, Popo Cole and Beau look over it. Reginald starts to dig, but it's too flooded from the storm to bury Celestine's body there. One more setback.

Cole marches them to the edge of the Bayou. The wind stops. There is only the sound of the rain.

Popo Cole loads the Landry-Boudreaux's and Goodman into his Pero boat. Johnny, the other shrimpers, and Reginald stay behind on shore with Father Gaudet. Just before the boat drives off, Father Gaudet lays his hand on Celestine's body, administers a final blessing: "The Christian community welcomes you, Daughter, with great joy. In its name, I claim you for Christ our Savior." He makes the sign of the cross over Celestine's body.

Popo Cole ferries them out to where he's built the tree house coffin, six feet above the ground.

Before the family puts Celestine there—into her final resting place—, Trent gives one of his Special Olympics medals to his mother. Cole gives up his medal of St. Christopher from his sock and puts both Trent's medal and his around Celestine's neck. Belle offers her necklace. Beau gives her a picture he carries in his wallet of him and Trent. Goodman, who has been carrying a carved rose quartz rosary in his pocket, blessed by the Pope himself, puts it in Celestine's hands.

Together, they all hoist the body up and load Celestine into Popo Cole's treehouse coffin.

Popo Cole nails the door shut.

Trent does the sign of the cross, "Father, Son, Holy Spirit Amen. Please tank you bery much."

They all sit together in the Pero for a moment of silent communion. Then, Popo Cole says, "I best go help some others on their rooftops." He ferries them safely back to shore where Reginald, Father Gaudet, Johnny and the other shrimpers wait.

Popo Cole takes in his family, each one, with a long and reverential gaze, his heart shining through his seasoned eyes. He silently nods to Goodman. Then, he turns back to the Bayou once again and disappears.

The sun peeks up over the horizon. And birds sing for Celestine.

Made in the USA
San Bernardino, CA
22 May 2016